ROBOT DEPOT

Russell F. Moran

Robot Depot
Coddington Press
Copyright © 2017 Russell F. Moran
Printed in the United States of America
ISBN (Print) 9780999000311
ISBN: 0999000314

DEDICATION

This book is dedicated to the inventors of the world.

ACKNOWLEDGEMENTS

As always, I thank my wife, Lynda, for her attentive reading and rereading of my many drafts, and for laughing at my jokes. I also thank my friend and copy editor, John White, for his proofreading and editing. And I especially thank my readers, many of whom are a constant source of inspiration and encouragement for me.

AUTHOR'S NOTE

You will find a **Cast of Characters** after the last chapter of the book. It can be frustrating to come across a character on page 150, who you first met on page 20, especially if you've put the book down for a few days. I've seen this done in Russian literature, and I happily add a cast of characters to *Robot Depot* as well as my other novels.

CHAPTER ONE

"This is the 911 Operator - Do you need police, fire, or ambulance? My name's Josie. How may I assist you?"

"It's my wife," the man screamed. "She's not breathing. She's totally non-responsive."

"Easy, honey. The calmer you are, the more I can help you. How old is your wife?"

"She's only 26. We got married last month. Please send help. She's not breathing."

"Just a couple of questions, sweetie, then I'll send the ambulance," operator Josie said.

"Do you have access to another cellphone?"

"Yes, my wife's phone is next to her," the man said, his voice clipped with impatience.

"Hold that phone next to her left temple, that's left, not right," Josie said.

"She can't fucking breathe. How the hell is she going to talk on the goddam phone?" the man yelled.

"Easy, baby, just do as I ask, okay? Is the phone next to the left side of her head?"

"Yes. Now what the hell do you want me to do?"

"I'm going to send a signal to the phone, honey. Just you relax and keep holding the phone next to her head."

The man heard a loud high pitched ringing sound coming from his wife's phone, followed by what sounded like three bird chirps.

His wife sat bolt upright and looked at him. "Hi honey, what are we doing on the floor?"

As soon as she said that, she collapsed into unconsciousness again.

"She sat up and spoke to me, but then she was out again," the man said.

"Now you listen to Josie, sweetie. Put that phone next to her head and keep it there for at least one hour. To make it easy on your arm, you may want to tape it there. Use masking tape if you have any. Do not use packing tape or you'll pull the poor thing's hair out when you remove it. I'm going to keep sending signals. Our equipment shows me that your wife's phone is fully charged."

The man sat with his back propped up by the kitchen table after he taped his wife's cellphone to her head.

"Jonesey, are you still there?" the man asked.

"The name's Josie, sweetie pie, I'm still here. I won't hang up until you tell me it's okay. We're here for you, baby."

"Josie, God bless you. Sorry about my rough language before, but I guess you're used to upset callers. I'm sitting here amazed. My wife wasn't breathing, but you sent a signal over the phone and she sprang to life. What do I do next?"

"She definitely needs a checkup, honey. What happened to her is not what's supposed to happen."

"I'm going to call our doctor right now. He has office hours tonight." The man said.

"No way, baby. Don't call a doctor. Here, take this number down although you probably have it already with the user's manual that you obviously didn't read. 1-800-BOT-DEPOT. That's the number for Robot Depot. Just explain to them what happened and they'll take care of everything."

"Josie, you're freaking me out. Why would I call Robot Depot about my wife?"

"Because that's where you bought her, sweetie."

CHAPTER TWO

"Like a complete asshole, in case you're wondering," Jenny said as she poured my wine.

My wife Jenny and I love to play a game with each other. We guess an answer to a question we think the other person is about to ask. Jenny seldom loses a round.

"I hope that isn't the answer to my question, 'How did I look on TV?' "

"*Yesss*, you nailed it, honey. I love you—in person. But on TV, let's face it, you suck."

"I wish you'd get to the point," I said.

"Very funny. Hey, Mike, look at you. Six feet tall, wonderful hair, blue eyes, great build. Hell, you're the sexiest man in the world, well *my* world. But on TV you look and talk like a total schmuck. And that costume they put you in, c'mon please. You look like a goddam robot."

"But that's the idea, hon—I'm supposed to look like a robot. Of course robots don't even look like robots anymore, so that's why they dressed me up like an 'old fashioned' robot. I'm supposed to be a throwback, get it? I'm supposed to look like one of those robots on Saturday morning kid's TV shows we used to watch. Remember when IBM came out with a personal computer? What character did they use in their ads? Charlie Chaplin, an old time silent comedian who had absolutely nothing to do with technology. He made the PC non-threatening, as he skipped along smelling a rose, happy as a lark because that little box just solved all of his business problems."

"So rather than dress you up to look like a doofus, why don't they just give you a flower to hold? I think you need an agent-ectomy."

"C'mon, Jen, Blanche is a hell of a talented lady. I interviewed a lot of agents before I picked her. And she's more than just an agent. She's a one woman talent agent, advertising exec, and public relations manager."

"Blanche! That's another thing," Jen said. "Here we are in the twenty-first century, and her friggin name is Blanche. I mean would you name a robot Blanche?"

"So you think I was dumb for hiring Blanche, and dumb for going with the ad agency she set me up with, and dumb for letting them dress me up like a robot?"

"Dumb?" Jenny said. "The last word I would ever put in a sentence with your name is 'dumb.' Mike, you're a goddam genius. *Forbes, Fortune, The Wall Street Journal.* I mean, holy shit, they don't write about dumb people, and they love you. Not as much as I do, but they think you're the best. You, Mike Bateman, the founder of Robot Depot, the most fabulous business idea in decades. You spotted a trend and got out in front of it. Hell, in five short years you've put Robot Depot in 30 states, and before long we'll be in every state. Because of you we have money coming out of our ears. You're one of the smartest people on the planet and Blanche's advertising clowns turned you into a robot out of the 1950s. And the words they put in your mouth make it sound like you're selling used cars."

When I talk business with Jenny, I wonder why I spend so much money on consultants. She's not just my partner, wife, and lover, but she's my number one advisor. Jen would never take credit for it, but you can see the impact of her ideas on every shelf at Robot Depot. Despite the money we're making, Jenny has kept her job as an engineering professor at Stony Brook University because she loves teaching and writing. I find it ironic that Jenny is a university professor because she has the mouth of a cab driver in traffic. When Jenny talks, I listen, especially when she starts the conversation by telling me I look like an asshole on TV.

Jen and I live in New York State in Islip, Long Island, which is part of the large suburban town of Islip, with a population of over 300,000 people. We actually live in the hamlet of Islip, populated by about 19,000 people, which is a small unincorporated part of the big Town of Islip. Islip, both town and hamlet, are located in Suffolk County, which is part of Long Island, which is not a political entity at all, much like the hamlet of Islip. And they say robotics is confusing. We live in a 10,000 square-foot house, nestled on three and a half acres on a beautiful creek that leads out to the Great South Bay. The bay isn't really a bay — it's a lagoon, but don't get me started. The property also includes a two bedroom, two bath guest house down by the creek. Although we deal every day with cutting edge technology innovations, Jen and I love old things, such as our house which was built in 1929. Because we don't have any kids, it's just the two of us rattling around in the big old mansion. With nine bedrooms and seven bathrooms we often entertain out-of-town friends and relatives. Given all that room in the house, you'd think we need a staff of servants to run the place. No problem, we have robots.

Jenny and I were both born and raised on Long Island. We love the place despite the traffic and insane real estate taxes. The home office of Robot Depot is located in Hauppauge, about eight miles from our house. It's also in the Town of Islip. Don't ask.

Hauppauge is a lively place for business. Besides our company's home office in Hauppauge, there are three Robot Depot stores on Long Island, one in Huntington, one in Mineola, and one near the home office in Hauppauge. Our main manufacturing facility is also on Long Island, in Hempstead. Jen and I also own a brownstone on East 86th Street in Manhattan, a useful place when I have to attend a meeting in the Big Apple.

"We're shooting another commercial next Tuesday," I said. "I picked that day because you don't have any classes, and I had a funny feeling that you'd like to meet Blanche. Also, I'll need help getting into my robot costume."

"I'll bring shears with me so I can cut that piece of shit into ribbons," Jenny said. She was about to say something else, when she blurted out, "what's that noise in the next room?'"

"That's our new floor cleaning bot." I said. "We've had him for three years, but I just had him outfitted with a speech module. I wanted you to see it before we make any decisions about stocking it."

"What's his name?" Jen asked. We always name our bots. Makes it feel, I don't know, less creepy. I would never say that to anybody, except Jen.

"His name is Dusty. Cute, no?" I asked. "Dusty, the bot that picks up dust."

"Yeah, right," Jen said as she rolled her eyes. Then she yelled toward the den, "Hey Dusty, do you mind? We're trying to have a fucking meeting in here."

"I'm sorry, madam," Dusty said. "I'll make note of where I left off and return to my station to await further activation."

"Thanks, Dusty," we both said. In my business, talking to machines comes second nature.

"No fucking problem," Dusty said.

"Excellent vocalization, honey," Jen said, "but you should clean up his language a bit."

7

"He comes equipped with a new advanced language learning chip," I said. "He picks up what he hears around him, including speech patterns and usage, and it becomes part of his database. He's been listening to you, obviously."

I always kid Jenny about her trash talking but oddly, it adds to her charm. I love her as much as the day we met 15 years ago, back in the days before Robot Depot. Our first encounter was under somewhat strange circumstances. I was a Marine captain and platoon leader in Afghanistan and Jenny was a lieutenant in charge of our battalion administrative quarters. We first saw each other soon after Jenny reported to the battalion. We met in the chow line during lunch. She was beautiful, which isn't easy to say about someone in Marine fatigues. She was, and is, extremely intelligent. Besides her engineering degree, she speaks fluent Arabic, something she picked up from a college roommate. Jen also managed to get an MBA from Yale before she joined the Marines. She's a real patriot, a trait she got from her parents, who had both served with the Marine Corps. We chatted briefly and shared some childhood recollections of Long Island, the place where we both grew up.

As we were talking, a bomb exploded at the other end of the mess hall, throwing debris and human body parts across the room. I was hit in the head by a flying piece of lumber and fell to the floor, still conscious but bleeding heavily. We heard shouts and saw a group of five enemy fighters rush into the building through the hole caused by the bomb. I reached for my pistol but I couldn't move my hand, which was injured when I fell. Jenny dropped to a knee on the floor next to me and opened fire with her M16, killing all five of the attackers. I was more than a bit impressed. Brains, beauty, and the willingness to kick ass when necessary. She visited me at the base hospital the next day, where I was recovering from my relatively minor wounds. We became good friends. If she wasn't engaged to be married, I would have worked on a serious relationship. A week later, Jenny received word that her fiancée, an Army lieutenant, was killed in a firefight at a base camp 20 miles from our headquarters. Jenny was given leave to arrange for her fiancé's body to be sent to his parents in the States. When she returned, our friendship continued, but nothing serious. Jenny was still grieving. By sheer coincidence, Jenny and I were scheduled to leave Afghanistan on the same plane after our tours were up. As we walked toward the C-130, two enemy fighters sprang from behind a building and opened fire. Jenny's rifle was slung over her shoulder, not in firing position. I swung my weapon free and shot the two attackers, killing both of them.

"I guess we owe each other," Jenny said when we boarded the plane. "Why," I said, "just because we saved each other's lives?" A combat zone makes for strange conversations. We lost track of each other, as often happens with comrades in arms. I thought about her a lot, but for some dumbass reason I never tried to reach out to say hello. I think Jenny's right; sometimes I'm an asshole.

About two years after mustering out of the Marine Corps, I was working as a marketing manager for Home Depot, and Jen was teaching engineering at Stony Brook University. Our paths crossed once again by total coincidence. We both attended a charity fundraiser for the St. Baldrick's Foundation, an organization that raises money to fight children's cancer. Like many of the participants, I shaved my head, and rounded up a bunch of friends and coworkers to chip in money because of my self-inflicted baldness. Bald— St. Baldrick, get it? We met at the buffet table and immediately recognized each other. "Hey, let's get a drink," Jen said. "You and I tend to get shot at while in line with each other."

"Don't look at me," I said, as we walked to the bar. "I look weird with my head shaved."

I couldn't *not* look at Jenny. The first time I saw her in Marine combat fatigues, she looked great, but now she was drop dead gorgeous, wearing a slightly short blue dress which highlighted her curves and her beautiful legs. Her light auburn hair emphasized her ice blue eyes.

"You did that for the kids?" She asked, pointing toward my bald crown.

"Yeah, I do it every year," I said.

"In that case, you don't look weird, you look wonderful," she said. "If I remember, you look impossibly sexy with a full head of hair."

"Did you say that sex is impossible?" I joked.

"Wiseass," she said. "Let's step outside for some fresh air. It's stuffy in here." She grabbed me by the hand.

So we had our fresh air, kissed for the first time, fell in love not long after that, and got married. We were both 30 years old. Of all the success I've enjoyed in life, meeting and falling in love with Jenny is the best. Even when she calls me foul names.

CHAPTER THREE

"Good afternoon everyone, and welcome to *Your World*. I'm your host, Neil Cavuto. We have a fascinating guest today, Mike Bateman, founder and CEO of the wildly successful chain of stores, Robot Depot. Mike's a guy who spotted a trend just five short years ago, and now in 2017 you can find Robot Depots in 30 states, and the way he's pushing the expansion button they'll soon be in every state. And the guy's only 38 years old. After Mike graduated from NYU, he entered the Marine Corps as a second lieutenant. After serving a tour in Iraq and one in Afghanistan, he mustered out of the Marines with the rank of captain and a chest full of medals for bravery, including a Purple Heart. Robot Depot stock trades on the New York Stock Exchange, and the arrow always seems to point up. A few years ago people discovered that a fast food joint, run properly, is almost recession-proof. Over the past few years we have had some serious market corrections, but Robot Depot keeps charging ahead. People are beginning to look at robots as they do hamburgers. Maybe you can do without them, but you sure as hell don't want to."

"Mike, welcome to our show. In preparing for this segment I visited one of your stores near my home in New Jersey. Full disclosure, folks—I now own Robot Depot stock. I need a better word than 'impressed,' more like amazed. Just like Andrew Carnegie, Steve Jobs, Bill Gates, and Jeff Bezos, you have a way of spotting what people want and giving it to them—whether they realize it or not. Mike, tell us a bit about Robot Depot."

"Thanks, Neil. I think a lot of business stories begin with 'One day my wife came home with a fill-in-the-blank.' The blank, in my case, was a robotic floor cleaner. Before you leave the house, you press a button, and the thing would scramble from room to room to pick up dust and debris. I saw what an enormous time-saver it could be, especially since one of my agreed-upon house chores was vacuuming the floors. The newer models not only clean your floor; they carry on a pleasant conversation with you as a result of our new language learning module. You don't need to press a button to start it up; you just give it a voice command. After we got our first floor cleaner, my curiosity went on high alert and I discovered that I had an entrepreneurial side. This robot idea is important, I thought, and it needs to be nurtured. My wife, Jenny and I had a great time making lists of actions that machines could perform as well as or better than human beings. At Robot Depot we now stock a robotic device for almost any chore you can imagine. We carry robotic lawn mowers – that are actually quite safe. We also carry robotic window washers, trash removal devices of various sizes, home security instruments, cooking equipment, laundry disposals, and paper shredders with timing reminders, just to name a few. Those things have been in our stores since the beginning. We now dedicate a special section of each store to drones. We carry fixed wing and helicopter drones, of course, but we also stock aquatic drones. A friend of mine has a son who picked golf balls out of water hazards as a part-time job while in college. He was once severely bitten by an alligator at a golf course in Florida. My friend invested in an aquatic drone that putters around water hazards, identifies golf balls, and picks them up with an arm extension. The drone can even sense when an animal approaches and lets out a loud chirp to scare the gator off. No sense using a drone that keeps getting its arms bitten off. Aquatic drones have been around a long time, for undersea exploration, for example. But now, inexpensive drones can be used for picking up golf balls, inspecting swimming pools for potential leaks, and just about any underwater task."

"Mike, what do you see as the next big thing on the horizon in robotics?" Cavuto asked.

"Our society is now rushing headlong into a world of driverless cars, which are no more than robots on wheels. People get nervous when they think of taking their hands off the wheel and giving control to a robot in the trunk, but studies show that robotic cars are better drivers than us humans. They don't text or check messages on their cell phones, for example. If somebody cuts the vehicle off, it doesn't curse and flash a middle finger. And robots don't drink or fall asleep at the wheel. Robot Depot is right there with the new car technology, and we expect to build robotic car dealerships as soon as we think the technology has been perfected."

"Mike," Cavuto said, "a lot of your company's literature discusses artificial intelligence, also known as 'AI.' The world was blown away a few years ago when the IBM artificial intelligence machine named *Watson*, also known as a 'question answering computer,' defeated two *Jeopardy* winners and won a grand prize of $1 million, which IBM donated to charity. IBM also developed the famous chess playing computer named *Deep Blue*, which defeated chess champion Gary Kasparov."

"We're as much in the artificial intelligence business as we are in robotics," I said. "The two areas often intersect, with the robot being the delivery end of an Artificial Intelligence computer. But somehow, we realized that Artificial Intelligence Depot was a lousy name for a chain of stores."

"What are some other activities where robots and AI are moving into?" Cavuto asked.

"Let me show you an example, Neil. Just read this aloud," I said, handing him a piece of paper,

Cavuto read: "Wisconsin appears to be in the driver's seat en route to a win, as it led 51-10 after the third quarter. Wisconsin added to its lead when Russell Wilson found Jacob Pedersen for an eight-yard touchdown."

"Doesn't sound like anything out of the ordinary, Mike," Cavuto said. One of the likeable things about Neil Cavuto is that he plays a great straight man.

"That article," I said, "according to *The New York Times*, was written within 60 seconds of the end of the game, typical of rapid response sports reporting. But what isn't typical is that it was written entirely by a computer."

Cavuto's mouth literally dropped. In preparing for this show, I didn't discuss with him that Artificial Intelligence computers can write.

"Mike, I'm speaking to you as a journalist. Are you saying that a computer can replace the writing efforts of a human being?"

"Yes, Neil, that's exactly what I'm saying, especially for subjects that are dependent on numbers, such as sports which I just showed you. Finance and investments are another area where Artificial Intelligence machines can take over. And studies show that AI computers are far more accurate than human beings."

"How about TV journalists," Cavuto asked, "folks like your charming and humble host? Can AI computers or robots take our place?"

"You raise an interesting question, Neil," I said. "It's probably the most important question of all when we're thinking about the future of AI and robotics. 'Can these machines replace that elusive idea of a personality?' Right now, and I mean *now* in the year 2017, the answer is no. Robots aren't sentient, and can do no more than mimic a human personality, including things like speech patterns and mannerisms, but no machine can replace a fully functional personality such as you."

"But Mike," Cavuto said, "you emphasized the words 'right now.' You seem to mean that sometime in the future we will see a robot that really acts like a human being. This seems to be a subject of science fiction, no?"

"Neil, a few years ago we would think a person was nuts if he said we could find a street address with help from a satellite in space communicating with a receiver in the dashboard of our car. Now, a GPS device is the way we get around, including getting directions while walking with our cellphones. Soon, driverless cars will just communicate with a satellite overhead and let you read the morning paper. So in answer to your question, yes, in the future we'll see robots that look and act like human beings."

"That brings us to a controversial subject, Mike," Cavuto said, "I've read reports of companies that are developing robots that look and feel like humans, and these robots are designed primarily for sex. Advances in cosmetic surgery have given us synthetic substances that feel like human skin. This medical technology is now being transferred to the realm of, and there's no better name for it, 'robotic sex.' Soon people will be able to purchase or rent a robot as a substitute for a sex partner. Can you comment on that?"

"Neil, Robot Depot, both as a manufacturer and as a retailer, is dedicated to making life easier for people, but that mission does not include easy sex. We're keeping a country mile away from those sex-bots as they're called. It's not what our company is about and it never will be."

"I'm glad to hear that, Mike. You've built a company that you can be proud of and it would be a shame to see you compromise your ethics and morals for a buck. To change the subject, I'd like to run a clip of a TV ad that Robot Depot is running in most market areas. I think it's hysterical, featuring you dressed up in a 1950s robot costume."

"Before you run the clip, Neil, I need to let you know that my top advisor is adamantly against that ad." Jenny's going to freak out over this, I thought.

"And who is your top advisor, Mike? Will we all recognize his or her name?"

"You'll recognize her, Neil. Jenny is the lady you met in the Green Room right before the show. Besides being my top advisor, Jenny is my wife, and still my girlfriend. Jenny sometimes speaks with a salty tongue, and she told me in no uncertain four letter words what she thought of me in a robot costume."

"Well, Mike, *my* top advisor—my producer—is screaming four letter words in my ear to run the clip. Let's see what our viewers think after we run a questionnaire on the show's website."

Cavuto ran the clip of my TV ad. Gotta admit, Jenny was right. The ad sucks. Cavuto laughed, but I think it was forced. I caught him wincing at a couple of points. The ad ended with me in my robot costume saying,

"Don't buy a bot until you check out Robot Depot, your *Bot People.*"

CHAPTER FOUR

"I thought you were great — in answer to the question you were about to ask me," Jenny said after she sipped her coffee. "Except for that clip of your dumb TV spot, I think the Cavuto show was one of your best appearances. You made me proud of you, honey, especially because you weren't dressed up like a fucking robot."

"I can't wait for you to meet Blanche tomorrow," I said. "She told me she's heard so much about you that she's dying to meet you."

"I hope she won't mind if I suggest that she change her name," Jenny said. "I mean, hey, *Blanche*?"

━◁+◁▷━

Jenny and I finished breakfast, cooked and served by Omelet, our new breakfast robot.

"Omelet, really knows how to cook, hon. We should have gotten her a long time ago."

"Thank you, madam," Omelet, said.

"Stop calling me madam, asshole."

"I'm pleased that you enjoyed breakfast, asshole," Omelet said.

"You've got to work on those new speech modules, Mike."

"You should watch your earthy tongue, Jen. You've convinced our window-washing bot that his name is 'dipshit.' Let's go, Blanche awaits us."

We got into our new Cadillac *Robette.* I think the model name is dumb, but it's one of the best robotic cars on the road, according to *Consumer Reports* and *Car and Driver.* Like all of our bots, we gave the car a name—*Carly*—get it? It was pouring rain, so I was happy to be chauffeured by a self-driving car, which is a better driver than me. We decided to meet at Blanche's office because she had all sorts of audio-visual equipment set up to show us different ad ideas. Blanche comes from an advertising background, so meeting with her usually involves a lot of photographs and film clips. I hoped that Jenny would like her. God knows she doesn't like her name.

Blanche almost ran out of her office to greet us in the hallway. She's best described as wiry, a sort of young Justice Ruth Bader Ginsberg. Her face is friendly and pleasant, kind of pretty but quite thin. According to the form she filled out before she signed the consulting contract, Blanche is 40 years old. She moves with such energy I swear I can see her leaving smoke behind her.

"Oh, my God," Blanche yelled—she yells a lot—"you must be Jenny. I'm so glad that Mike didn't marry a robot."

"As I've mentioned to you, Blanche, Jenny is my top advisor, in every way. She has some questions about the Robot Depot TV ad with me dressed like a robot."

"Wow, does that ad suck," Blanche said. "I think we should pull it from every market. Come into our taping room where I can show you some new ideas."

Jenny didn't say anything, but I could tell by her smile that she was starting to like Blanche. Maybe she'd even learn to tolerate her name.

"I saw you on Cavuto yesterday," Blanche said. "I thought the show was great, except for that piece of shit clip of your robot commercial."

Jenny just made a new friend, I thought.

"I want to pull you out of doing ads and concentrate on booking you on more shows like Neil Cavuto's," Blanche said. "Jenny, I'm sure you've noticed that you have an extremely handsome husband."

"Yes, I have noticed that, Blanche, especially when he's not dressed up like a robot."

Jenny actually called Blanche by her name. A good sign.

"No way in hell are we going to cover up this good-looking guy in a dumb costume," Blanche said. "He drives up Robot Depot stock just being interviewed by a good host like Cavuto. I want to concentrate more on that from a PR point of view, not advertising. There are plenty of good actors out there who can do humor as well as pitch products. Mike's not one of them. He's a great executive, not a great comedian."

"Blanche, I'm so happy we're on the same page," Jenny said. "I hated that robot costume."

"I'm glad to say it wasn't my idea. Some kid in our not-so-aptly-named creative department came up with it. He's the CEO's nephew. Please accept my apologies."

"No problem, Blanche," Jenny said, "I knew that couldn't have been your idea."

These two are definitely becoming pals, I thought.

Blanche spun around in her chair and yelled to someone in the corner of the office. "Hey, Buzz, bring us that bag of pretzels."

Buzz buzzed over our heads and neatly placed the bag of pretzels on the table. Buzz is a small helicopter drone, four inches in diameter.

"Buzz looks like one of ours," I said.

"Of course it's one of yours," Blanche said. "Do you think I buy bots from just anyone?"

If Blanche were an artist she'd be a performance artist. She popped a pretzel into her mouth, took a swig from a bottle of water, folded her hands and looked at me with a face that announced that she had something important to say.

"I need to ask you something, Mike. On the Cavuto show, the subject of sex-bots came up. You told him that Robot Depot would have nothing to do with them. I'm asking this question as your PR lady. Is it definite that you won't carry those damn sex-bots?"

"Absolutely so," I said. "I've invested too much time, effort, and money into this company to trash its reputation. We're investing in android-looking figures like you see at Disney World, but only for non-controversial uses such as greeting people and giving directions. You may have noticed the one in the lobby of our home office, that tall guy wearing a butler uniform who says, 'Welcome to Robot Depot.' He's not a guy, he's a bot."

"Holy shit! I flirted with him the last time I was at your office. What's his name?"

"Dick," I said.

"I'll leave it at that," Blanche said. "But it illustrates my point. If that friggin machine attracted a lonely divorcee, imagine what those sex-bots can do. Do not trash the reputation of your fine company with sex machines, Mike. What do you call those kind of robots anyway? They look so human."

"As a general term, they're called androids or humanoids. We like to call them *hubots*, short for humanoid robots," I said. "Besides being useful as greeters, they can be programmed with a large vocabulary. Imagine a TV weatherman who gives weather updates every half hour. A TV station can buy one of those *hubots* for around $100,000, which is nothing compared to the annual salary of an experienced weather reporter. The bot takes no vacation, never calls in sick, receives no salary, doesn't make moves on the boss's wife, and doesn't make mistakes."

Blanche was furiously taking down notes. She had this quaint old-fashioned way of jotting things on a yellow pad rather than tapping into a phone device.

"Looks like you've got some ideas, Blanche," Jenny said.

"You bet I do," Blanche said. "I want to start booking Mike to speak at big conventions. If he explains to budget-minded executives what he just explained to us about the weatherman bot, I can see new markets springing open. Mike, I'm going to put together a presentation that will knock your socks off. Can we get together next week? Please bring Jenny along. I love her ideas."

The attendant in the building lobby of Blanche's office typed a few numbers into a keypad and Carly, our robocar, drove to the front door to pick us up. Jenny was coming to my office with me after we stopped for lunch.

"So what did you think about Blanche, hon?"

"She's wonderful, just like you said, Mike, and I can even live with her name. That woman is a nonstop explosion of great ideas. When she said that your robot costume wasn't her idea, I realized I had a new friend."

"I want you to be there for her presentation next week" I said. "When Blanche gets excited she puts on a show you don't want to miss."

"I'll definitely be there," Jen said. "Hey, let's go to a nice place for dinner tonight. I have something big to tell you about."

CHAPTER FIVE

We walked into Mario's at six, right after we left the office. Mario's, located less than a mile from our headquarters, is our favorite restaurant. Whenever Jen and I make reservations, the owner himself always greets us if he's there. I think he appreciates all of the corporate functions we host at the place. Mario showed us to our favorite table in the back of the room.

"So what's the big announcement, hon." I said. "You've kept me wondering for hours. Tell me that they made you a full professor."

"I think you should set me up with a nice office, preferably one with a window overlooking the garden," Jen said. "No, I haven't been named a full professor. I'm now officially an adjunct, with no more than one course assigned to me. I've decided that Robot Depot is a lot more exciting than Stony Brook University. You've been trying to entice me with the title Vice President for Product Development. Well, honey, I've decided to accept your offer. Now think about a nice office for me."

I'm not a particularly demonstrative man, but suddenly I felt like doing a handstand on the table. Jenny as a full time vice president with Robot Depot is something I've dreamed about. I stood, walked around the table and planted a kiss on Jen's lips.

"I have a feeling like I had when you accepted my marriage proposal," I said. "You've made my day, if not my year. Is it okay if I say 'I love you,' to my newest executive?"

"You certainly may," Jen said. "I don't have to call you 'sir,' do I?"

I laughed. I asked our waiter to bring Mario to the table.

"Mario, meet the newest vice president at Robot Depot."

He whispered something to the waiter. Five minutes later Mario appeared with an expensive bottle of champagne. He joined us in a toast to the best news that Robot Depot has gotten in years.

CHAPTER SIX

Two days later Carly drove Jen and me to our private jet hangar at Long Island MacArthur Airport in Ronkonkoma. We were tired from celebrating Jenny's early retirement from Stony Brook last night. With all of the exciting things happening at Robot Depot, Jenny finally realized that our company was a bigger part of her life than teaching classes, and much more exciting. I suggested that, in addition to new product development, Jenny take on the job of overseeing the training of new employees. Professor Jenny loved the idea.

"So after you've had a night to sleep on it, are you still happy about your decision to leave Stony Brook?"

"What sleep, honey? We screwed our brains out all night. Don't you remember?"

"Yes, I do remember," I said as I stroked her thigh.

"Is everything okay back there?" Carly asked.

"Hey, Carly, just keep your fucking eyes on the road," Jenny suggested.

We pulled up next to the hangar where the Robot Depot Gulfstream G650 was parked. Some members of my board questioned whether the Gulfstream was a bit extravagant, but when we looked at the numbers they made sense. It is expensive, at $65 Million, but the plane is so popular we could sell it used at a profit. That made our financial VP happy, because the high current value meant that the plane hardly caused a ripple on our balance sheet. The G650 can fly eight passengers and four crew 7,000 nautical miles non-stop, and has a maximum speed of mach .925, almost the speed of sound, making it the fastest commercial jet in service. Jenny and I named the plane *Skybot*, pretty lame if you ask me, but kind of appropriate. Automation has been a part of the aircraft industry since flight began, and *Skybot* was no exception. The jet is filled with robot-like amenities, which naturally attracted me, such as voice-activated dashboard on the back of each seat, showing TV, speed, weather, and ETA.

Our destination was Dulles Airport in Washington, D.C. At lunchtime we were scheduled to meet with General Bill Clark, Chief of Procurement for the United States Army. General Bill and I hit it off a few years ago when we first met. We both served in Afghanistan at the same time, although in different parts of the country. Bill told me that he preferred to do business with people who were combat veterans. He said that it gave the dealer a mental stake in what he sold to the Army and he's right. Having seen the results of well-made military robots as well as occasional pieces of shit, I really do care about what we sell to the armed forces. The general was also impressed that Jenny was a Marine veteran too. Our meeting would address our new line of ground combat robots. Most of what we sell to the Department of Defense are aircraft drones, but this would be an infantry robot. It was a project that fascinated Jenny, and she informally headed up the development, even though she wasn't employed by Robot Depot at the time.

General Bill is approaching 55 years old, and will be retiring soon. He's a long-distance runner and stays in excellent shape. It would be totally unethical, even illegal, for me to make him a job offer, but that's exactly what I intend to do when he retires and is no longer in a position to buy our products. I want his expertise in developing robotic weapons systems.

A car took us from the Pentagon to a new DOD weapons testing facility in rural Maryland. It was originally located in the Baltimore-Washington metropolitan area, but a shit storm of protests arose over the constant sounds of explosions.

Ground combat robots are nothing new in the military. The German Army used remote- controlled vehicles named Goliath at the Battle of Normandy as well as other operations.

Robot Depot has been working on a new type of vehicle that is close to the ground, unlike the familiar robots with a tall periscope on top of an army tank-like vehicle. The taller robot is still necessary for surveillance and targeting activities, but our new model, called a *Groundhog*, is meant for demolition and attack. *Groundhog* is six inches high, two feet across, and weighs 75 pounds. I had shown the bot to Jenny a few weeks ago. Typical of Jen, she learned everything about the machine, and even made recommendations for improvements. And that was before she even worked at Robot Depot. General Bill, Jenny, and I sat on a reviewing stand with earphones on our heads. By the press of a button we could talk to each other rather than having to take the earphones on and off whenever we blew up a bot. The robot's name was Fred, a name chosen by Jenny.

"Why Fred?" asked the General.

"Because it rhymes with dead," Jenny said, "which will be the status of the enemy when Fred does his thing."

"General, I'm going to let Jenny, our Product Development VP, handle the demonstration. She knows our machines inside and out and knows how to explain the smallest detail."

Jenny sat with the remote console in her lap.

"This is one of the things we're going to change, General," Jenny said. "This console is much too big. It should fit into a soldier's backpack for immediate use."

She then pressed a button and the bot came charging through the simulated village. We definitely picked a good name for the model, because it did look like a groundhog scrounging around for food.

The general raised his hand and Jenny pressed a button to stop Fred.

"The strange thing I notice is that the sound from the machine seems to be coming from a spot 50 feet away in the opposite direction," General Bill said.

"That's a new device we're perfecting, General," Jenny said. "Almost like a ventriloquist, the sound from the machine gets sent in different directions at different times to confuse the enemy. We didn't want to dampen the sound because that would also decrease its power and speed, so we came up with this multi-directional sound device to make it difficult for the enemy to know where the sound is coming from."

"Wow," General Bill said. "The thing's also fast as hell."

"Earphones on guys," Jenny said.

She maneuvered Fred in and out of various obstacles and then next to a small house when she pressed another button. The sound of the explosion was so loud it hurt our ears even with the earphones on. The house was now a pile of smoking rubble.

"These *Groundhog* model machines, such as Fred, are designed for urban combat," I said, "as we've just seen. But, because of its weight and speed, it's also useful for attacking tanks, trucks and cars. They're also handy for dropping in on a meeting of the enemy."

"As I'm looking at this Fred thing do its work," General Bill said, "I'm thinking not just how many of the enemy we can kill, but how many American lives we can save. It would take a 16-man platoon to do what that robot just did, at maybe a 50 percent casualty rate."

"So you're pleased with our work, General?" Jenny said.

"Pleased? I want you to ship 1000 of those machines to our procurement depot as soon as possible. How fast will it take to re-design the remote console?"

"About a week, General. We've been working on it already." Jenny said.

"As soon as you're done, send them," General Bill said. "I'll have my assistant email you an order form. These robots can make a big difference in our current theaters of operation, especially after the troop cutbacks. Mike, Jenny, as usual you people have come through with what we need."

We dropped General Bill at the Pentagon, and Sergeant Jim drove us to Dulles.

After we got into our seats on the Gulfstream, Jenny made an observation.

"Mike, did you notice that the general didn't ask about price? He just ordered 1000 machines and his only concern was date of delivery. It's like he gave us a blank check."

"We're taxpayers too, hon," I said. "It's good to see taxpayer money going to something valuable. At $3,500 each, the total bill will come to $3.5 million. That's money well spent, if you ask me."

After the pilot turned off the seatbelt sign, I walked over to Jenny's seat, bent over and kissed her. "We've been a team for a long time," I said. "but watching you today in front of General Bill made me proud as hell. Have I mentioned recently how much I love you?"

"Hey, handsome, we have to maintain our membership-in-good-standing with the mile-high club," she said softly. "The de-signers of this jet were kind enough to provide a lovely bedroom. Let's go there—*NOW.*"

CHAPTER SEVEN

The day after our visit to the Pentagon, Carly dropped Jen and me in front of the Robot Depot building. Phil Townsend, head of the legal department, greeted us at the door.

"Phil, what's up?" I said. "You look like you're upset about something."

"Mike, I probably should have called to warn you about this, but I know that you like to face problems and get them over with. Hi, Jenny. Some nut case showed up about a half hour ago with his attorney. I know the lawyer, Jim Brody. Jim's a good guy and doesn't take on bullshit clients, but I think he made an exception with this creep. His client, John Beekman, is raving on about having bought a defective *hubot* from Robot Depot."

"That's weird," I said. "We've just gotten into the corporate greeter market and we haven't sold more than a dozen, and we sold them to big companies. I think we've only sold one female looking bot."

"Do you want to see him, Mike, or should I just call security?"

"No, let's get this over with," I said. "I want to know what's going on with this guy."

"They're in the second-floor conference room."

When Jenny, Phil, and I walked in, Jim Brody, the attorney, sprang to his feet.

"Thank you for agreeing to see us, Mr. Bateman. It's an honor to meet you," Brody said. "As I explained to Mr. Townsend of your legal department, my client, John Beekman here, has a problem he wants to discuss. I thought it would be appropriate if we could meet informally and maybe iron this out. John, please tell these folks what happened."

Beekman was a short skinny guy with thick glasses and a balding head. He wore an expensive suit. He sat at the table across from us folding and unfolding a napkin, and never once making eye contact with any of us.

"The problem I want to talk about concerns my wife," Beekman said.

"Your wife?" I said. I looked at his lawyer who just rolled his eyes, wearing an expression that said, "How did I wind up with a client like this?"

"Please go on, Mr. Beekman," I said. I was more than curious to see what this guy was up to.

"I came home last week and my wife was lying unconscious on the kitchen floor. She wasn't breathing and was unresponsive."

"I'm sorry to hear that. Is she okay?" I said, trying to figure out what the hell my company had to do with his sick wife.

"Well, let me tell you what happened," Beekman said. "I called 911 and the operator surprised me when she asked me to hold a phone to my wife's head. I just followed instructions and put my wife's cellphone to her head. My wife sat up and acknowledged me, and then collapsed again. The 911 operator told me that I should put the phone next to my wife's head and tape it there for an hour. While this was going on I asked the operator what I should do next. She said I should take my wife to Robot Depot. 'Why should I bring her to Robot Depot?' I asked the operator. 'Because that's where you bought her,' the operator said."

"You married a fucking robot?" Jenny inquired, a bit loudly.

"I didn't know she was a robot. We met about two months ago. She swept me off my feet, if I may be so dramatic. She's a beautiful woman, person, bot, whatever. I did not buy her at Robot Depot. I didn't buy her anywhere. I just married her."

"Where did you get the idea that she came from Robot Depot?" asked Phil Townsend.

"The 911 operator said that she could tell from the signal my wife put out when I placed the phone next to her head. So I went to the Robot Depot in Huntington. The guy at the counter said that you don't sell 'sex-bots' at Robot Depot. The son of a bitch actually called my wife a sex-bot. According to the serial number on her, she came from Robot Depot."

I bit my lip to keep from laughing at this nut. Phil Townsend, God bless him, called for a break so he could have a private chat with Mr. Beekman's attorney. They stepped out of the room.

"Pardon me but I have to puke, I mean pee," Jenny said as she walked to the ladies room.

"Jim, your client doesn't need a lawyer," Townsend said, "he needs a psychiatrist. Even if we sold sex-bots, which we don't, what the hell is he talking about? So the goddam thing's batteries went low. All he had to do was recharge it and he's got his 'wife' back, if not his sanity. Bottom line, Jim, is that we've only sold 12 of what we call *hubots*, short for humanoid robots, and only one of them was a female model. Companies use them for greeting people and various other simple functions like giving directions. With all of the services they give, sexual relations aren't among them. Mike Bateman enforces a corporate policy not to sell sex-bots—yes, that's what they're called, with all apologies to your client's imaginary wife. Even if the signal that the 911 operator found was from us, it doesn't prove a thing. Cut this bozo loose, Jim. He's not worth your time or reputation. Somebody has played a weird practical joke on this clown, and he's looking for somebody to blame."

The lawyers concluded that the meeting should end. Mr. Beekman returned home, presumably to his fully charged spouse. You can't make this shit up.

CHAPTER EIGHT

Blanche, Jenny, and I were having coffee in my office and catching up on the latest news on TV. Our coffee-making bot, Joe (as in cup of *joe*) wheeled up to us with a fresh pot of coffee. He not only makes excellent coffee, he delivers it.

"Holy shit, look at that," Blanche said, looking at the TV. "Another goddam near-riot demonstration. The poor anchorman isn't sure what the hell they're demonstrating about. We seem to live in a time where you just grab a sign and go out and shout. Oh wait, there's a sign. 'Hell No—We won't go, P.S. Nine has got to stay.' It seems that they're protesting the closing of a school."

"School closings always get people upset," I said.

"But those demonstrators are bent on violence. I just saw a guy get hit over the head with a sign." Jenny said. "Over a school closing?"

"Line one for you, Mike. He says he's George Clayton, the Police Commissioner of New York City," said Francine, my robot receptionist.

"It's nice to get a call from somebody who isn't a reporter," I said as I picked up the phone.

"Good morning, Mr. Commissioner, Mike Bateman here. Two senior executives are here with me. Is it okay if I put you on speaker? With me are Jenny Bateman, my wife and Vice President for Product Development, and Blanche Whiteacre, our public relations consultant."

"Go ahead and put the phone on speaker," Commissioner Clayton said. "This conversation may be sensitive but nothing top secret. If you've been watching the news lately, you may have noticed that demonstrations are getting out of hand. We're almost at a point where a teacher gets picketed for giving a kid a bad grade. Hey, that's what democracy is all about, but the NYPD has a problem, a big problem. We can barely staff up our existing manpower to keep up with the constant demonstrations. The Constitution won't let me stop them, but I sure as hell need some help in controlling them. I'm on Long Island for a funeral which just ended. Mind if I stop by your office? I can be there in thirty minutes."

"We'd be honored, Mr. Commissioner," I said. "See you in a half-hour."

"Yesss," Blanche screamed in her reticent way. "The friggin City of New York. Now that's a customer."

"He's talking about help with riots," Jen said. "We already stock machines that can help with crowd control. If my memory serves me, I think we've sold a few to the NYPD."

The receptionist showed Commissioner Clayton into my office. He's a big, burly guy in his early 60s I'd guess. He actually reminded me of the Tom Selleck character on the show *Blue Bloods*, right down to the three-piece suit and mustache. Joe, the coffee bot, wheeled up next to him with a fresh mug of coffee.

He insisted that we call him George and dispense with "commissioner." I told him to call us by our first names. The guy was polite as hell, and quite articulate. I guess he leaves the "tough cop" persona to his subordinates.

"Folks, as I indicated on the phone, there's a growing problem of violent demonstrations in New York. What's the difference between a violent demonstration and a riot? It depends on the journalist reporting the story. Point is, I'm talking about large groups of angry people, or people acting like they're angry. We've used and continue to use some of your excellent machines, but usually for bomb and hostage situations, occasions where I don't want to send in my cops. But it's getting worse every week as you can see from the news reports. It's complicated by the fact that a lot of demonstrators don't know what they're demonstrating for or against. So I have two objectives, to keep people from being injured or killed, and to protect my cops from the same fate. I'm trying to figure out solutions, but so far haven't come up with anything. You people have a reputation for excellent robotic solutions to violent problems."

"George, we've sold enough robots to the military to blow up everybody in New York City," I said, "but if I understand you correctly, you just want to put a stop to the violence, not to kill the bad guys."

"How about marbles?" Jenny said.

"But marbles can become weapons," I said.

"Jenny, are you suggesting that we may want to throw marbles at the feet of demonstrators?" Clayton said. "That's been tried by governments the world over. But just as Mike said, marbles can become weapons. We've seen it happen when it was tried years ago. So as far as ideas go, let's lose our marbles."

We all laughed politely at his lame joke.

"I don't think Jenny meant marbles literally, just as a concept," Blanche said.

"Thanks, Blanche," Jenny said. "Yes, that's exactly what I mean, the concept of marbles means something you slip and fall over.

We sure as hell know how to make hardened robots. Look at the stuff we send to the military. They don't break down till they blow themselves up. I'm not thinking about an explosive bot, just one that's low to the ground, moves fast, and is too heavy to pick up and throw at somebody. We can call it a 'marble bot.' Think about our *Groundhog* attack robot that we sell to the Army. The thing is low to the ground, moves like a scared rat, and will trip anyone in its way. Of course that bot is really a robotic bomb, but the idea is the same. Something low, heavy, and fast. It can be controlled remotely, of course, because we don't want the thing tripping the wrong people."

"Great," I said. "Let's put that on our product development list and we'll brainstorm it with the engineers."

"And let's not forget good old helicopter drones," Blanche said. "The problem with tear gas is that you can see the canister coming. How about we put a substance into a bunch of drones that makes people sneeze. It's hard to be violent if you're sneezing your brains out." Blanche has been morphing from PR executive to a key member of our creative team, and we just saw the new her in action.

"Let me propose this," I said. "We'll go into hard core creative mode and brainstorm the hell out of the ideas we've come up with as well as stuff we haven't thought about yet. George, give us two weeks and then we'll make a presentation of our ideas, showing you the good and bad points for each possibility."

Commissioner George left, with a big smile on his face, a lot happier than when he first showed up. I was thinking about the other applications we might have for just the two ideas we discussed. "Marble Bot?" Great idea.

CHAPTER NINE

"Good evening ladies and gentlemen, I'm Matt Stroud, your host for our new show, *The Book*. I've got some great news. When our show first hit the air last month, a lot of pundits said it would never make it. People are reading fewer books, so why would they want to watch a TV show all about reading books? Well, the public is proving the pundits wrong. Our ratings, I'm happy to report, are through the roof. The first segment for tonight's show, as we've done for the past few weeks, is all about a book that was chosen by our panel of readers. It's a debut novel by author Nigel Weill entitled *Opening the Frontier*. The 488-page book has gotten rave reviews and hit *The New York Times Best Seller Fiction List* at number one. Let's see what our distinguished panel thinks about this debut novel. Mary Patterson, professor of history at Columbia University, will kick off the segment."

"It's hard to believe that this is Weill's debut novel," Mary Patterson said. "After I read the book I thought, 'Where has this guy been?' The novel is a perfect blend of historical fiction, taking up on Frederick Jackson Turner's thesis of the closing of the

American frontier, along with some wild science fiction in the form of time travel. His characters are perfectly developed and the plot gallops along at a wonderful pace. I give this book five stars."

"Hi, I'm Jim Fleist, a best-selling novelist if I do say so myself, and a big fan of other novelists. I warn anybody who reads this wonderful book to take some Dramamine before reading it because the plot twists feel like a roller coaster. I just can't believe this is his debut novel. The author is a new star on the literary horizon, and I can't wait for his next book."

Stroud introduced a total of six panelists, all of whom raved about Nigel Weill's book.

"Although I'm the host," Stroud said, "I have to weigh in and say that I agree with our all-star panel. *Opening the Frontier* is one great book. From characters to plot, to subplots, to a dynamite ending, I loved this book. It sounds trite to say, but I couldn't put it down. I have a surprise for our panelists, however, as well as for our viewing audience. I'll spring the surprise right after this brief commercial break."

⋡⋦ ⋧⋫

"Welcome back to *The Book*, ladies and gentlemen. Before the break I promised you a surprise and I won't keep you waiting. This wonderful book that we've been discussing was not written by a human being."

A natural showman as well as a book lover, Stroud kept his mouth shut and let his words linger—"not written by a human being."

The camera surveyed the faces of the panelists after he said that. Pure confusion and disbelief. If a caption was placed on the screen it would be, "What did he just say?"

"*Opening the Frontier,*" ladies and gentlemen, was written 100 percent by a robot, an artificial intelligence computer named

Angus, developed by the AI and robot giant, Robot Depot. The name Nigel Weill is a pseudonym. I hope none of our panelists feel embarrassed, because I was right there with them. I thought the book was wonderful and I enjoyed reading every word of it. I only wish we could interview the author, but how do you interview a machine?"

"Was this Angus machine given an outline to work from?" Mary Patterson asked.

"I'm told that the robot was given only one thing, the title," Stroud said. "After that, there was no human intervention. Angus wrote the book, cover to cover. And get this. He did his own research, proofreading, line editing, and developmental editing."

"I feel like the earth has just shifted under my feet," said Pat Morgan, one of the panelists. "I'm trying to figure out what this means. What are the ramifications of a robot writing a book, not to mention performing all of the normal editorial services? What does it mean for agents and acquisition editors? What does it mean for the entire publishing industry?"

"Ladies and gentlemen, the publishing industry has gone through enormous changes in the past few years, beginning with the Kindle electronic reader and the explosive growth in self-published books. But those changes are nothing compared to what we've heard tonight. We're about out of time, but let me say this. I'm the host of a book show, and therefore I don't like to say overly dramatic things. However, I think it's fair to say that tonight we've seen a new page in the history of literature."

CHAPTER TEN

"Welcome to *The Book*, ladies and gentlemen. I'm your host, Matt Stroud. *The Book* is your show to watch for everything and anything concerning the wonderful world of books. Whether they're paperback, hardcover, or electronic, books make the world go around. We're calling last week's program *The Show that Freaked out the World*. We're calling it that because it's the truth. We freaked out the world, including your humble host. A big part of the show is on YouTube, so if you missed it, check it out. On that show our panel of experts reviewed a debut novel by a Mr. Nigel Weill. All six panelists loved the book, and so did I. It's number one on *The New York Times Bestseller List*. Not bad for a debut novel. But, as I announced to the about-to-be-freaked-out world that night, the wonderful book, *Opening the Frontier*, was written by a robot, an artificial intelligence computer named Angus. Nigel Weill is the machine's pseudonym. The only information that Angus was given was the title of the book. A lot of people didn't believe it and some still don't. My announcement, as I said, signaled a new page in the history of literature.

"We have a special guest on tonight's show, a man who is world famous, the CEO of Robot Depot, the company that created the robot which (or should I say *who?*) wrote the book. Mike Bateman will tell us about the future of publishing as he sees it. Welcome to *The Book*, Mike, and tell us a bit about the new world we find ourselves in."

"Thanks for inviting me to your show, Matt." I said. "Like you, we've received mountains of mail, both paper letters and email. Some people see us as an evil force out to ruin civilization. I see us as the opposite, a positive force out to improve our lives. I think that budding novelists are especially upset. So a guy sits at his desk and figures, 'here I am near the end of my first novel which I hope will be a big success, and along comes a damn robot and beats me to the finish line.' But I invite people to see the positive side of this event. Angus, the machine that wrote the book, is a natural out-growth of the science of artificial intelligence or AI. We've read all about *Watson*, the IBM computer that defeated two high winning *Jeopardy* contestants, and *Deep Blue*, another IBM computer that de-feated chess champion Garry Kasparov. Our development team that created Angus did much the same thing that the IBM pro-grammers did. We poured an enormous amount of information into the program, including texts about the art of writing novels. A novel has a structure, and numerous studies have been done on just how that structure should be followed, with plenty of leeway, of course, for creativity. It's the same with TV sitcoms. They fol-low a pattern, and good writers know the successful patterns and follow them. How about crime novels, where the detective tries to convince the chief detective to let him find the bad guy? The chief detective gives him 48 hours to find the villain, rescue the kid, or stop an explosion. These are patterns that we see over and over. Stephen King said that stories are like fossils, and the writer's job is to unearth them. So think of Angus as a fossil hunter. He—I can't help calling Angus by the personal pronoun—found a wonderful fossil in the *Opening the Frontier,* and made the most of it, just as any good novelist would. So the creation of Angus isn't a negative event for anybody, including writers. I'm going to predict that Angus will result in better writing from real live authors. If it's okay with you, Matt, I'd like to make the announcement about the upcoming joint effort between your show, *The Book,* and Robot Depot."

"Mike we're going to take a commercial break and then make the big announcement."

A small robot wheeled before the camera and said, "Don't touch the dial folks, because you're about to hear some exciting news. We'll be back shortly."

⊨⊰ ⊱⊨

After the commercial break, the announcement robot again wheeled up to the camera.

"Welcome back, folks. Let's hear it for our host Matt Stroud. He's a real human being."

Stroud leaned over to Mike Bateman and whispered, "This fucking robot is becoming a pain in the ass."

"Hey, it was your producer's idea."

"Welcome back to *The Book,* friends. If you're just joining us, the handsome fellow to my right is none other than Mike Bateman, CEO of Robot Depot. He spoke about the amazing AI machine they developed called Angus, a machine that wrote a best-selling novel. Mike is now going to tell us about an exciting joint venture between Robot Depot and our show. I've been told in confidence that the plan does not include replacing your charming host with a robot. Mike, tell us the news."

"Matt, as I was saying before the break, we at Robot Depot see the advent of a novel-writing robot as a positive development, and not one that will replace budding novelists out there. We're planning a month-long competition called *Write the Book.* Most new novelists are familiar with the annual NaNoWriMo, which stands for National Novel Writing Month, an event that runs through the month of November. The idea is to write the first draft of a novel, at least 50,000 words, during that month. You can check your progress on their website. *Write the Book* will be similar, with one big exception. The participants will be in groups of 50, and each group will include one writing robot. After the initial month, each participant will have another month to rewrite the first draft. At the end of the second month, all participants are encouraged to submit a completed manuscript electronically. Robot Depot will then submit all of the manuscripts to the acquisitions editor at the top five publishing houses. Whether the manuscript was written by a human being or a robot will not be disclosed to the publishers. Sixty days after submission, the publishing companies will select as many manuscripts as they desire to publish, along with a publishing contract for the author. Because the publishers can go forward with as many books as they want, the participants don't have to worry about a robot walking off with the only prize."

"Mike we have a question from a caller on line one. Go ahead, Bill from Rochester."

"Who designed this competition, Robot Depot or *The Book?*"

"Over 90 percent of the idea is from the people who produce this TV show." I said. "Robot Depot doesn't know a lot about publishing, so that's why we've teamed up with these folks. I should add that if one or more of our robots wins publishing contracts, we will donate all advances and royalties to creative writing programs at universities to be announced."

"Janice Newcomb from New Jersey is on line two," Stroud said. "Go ahead, Janice."

"Where do literary agents fit into all of this?" she asked. "It seems like a manuscript is going from the author to the publisher without an agent in the middle."

"Authors without agents are nothing new," I said. "The explosion of self-publishing over the past few years has nailed that concept. Will there be a future for literary agents when acquisition editors get used to receiving manuscripts directly from authors? Only time will tell. If the growth of novel writing continues, publishers are going to need help from experienced agents just to wade through the manuscripts."

"The competition begins next month, so start brainstorming on your next story," Stroud said. "That's all for tonight, folks. I'll sign off by saying, *Write the Book.*"

CHAPTER ELEVEN

"Mayday, Mayday, Mayday, this is the trawler *Andiamo* five miles off the coast of North Carolina, near Cape Hatteras," the boat captain yelled into his radio. He then read the coordinates of *Andiamo's* position.

"This is Coast Guard Cutter *Wilson*, Captain Peters speaking. Read you loud and clear, *Andiamo*. What's the problem, Captain?"

"I have a single engine and it's crapped out. I can't get it to start. The wind and waves are picking up like a bitch, and I'm worried that we'll capsize."

"This is the *Wilson*. I'm about five miles from your position, too far to get there in a hurry. The wind is gusting to 50 mph, which is too high for a helicopter from Hatteras. If you carry a sea anchor, deploy it now. I'm sending two helicopter drones. Both will be carrying flotation devices that you'll need to attach to the sides of your boat. The drones can't get too close to you but can fly accurately right above you. Tell us when you see them and keep reporting their position relative to your boat."

Drones are absolute life savers, thought the Coast Guard captain. He would never risk a helicopter in such high winds, for fear of losing the lives of its crewmen. But if a drone goes down, the only thing lost is the price of the drone, not a human life.

"*Wilson*, this is *Andiamo*. Your drones are in sight. Recommend you raise them about ten feet and send the first one over us."

The drone pilot on the *Wilson* eased the first drone forward, following instructions from the captain of *Andiamo*. He positioned the drone right above the trawler and released the flotation devices. The captain of *Andiamo* and three passengers grabbed the devices and attached them to the rails of the boat, tying them down to deck cleats. No sooner had they attached the flotation balloons when a huge wave crashed broadside into *Andiamo*'s starboard hull. The boat hardly listed, held steady by the flotation gear.

"Please send the next drone to drop the rest of the floats as insurance," *Andiamo*'s captain said. "The first batch saved our lives."

The second delivery landed in the middle of the deck and the crew secured the floaters to any spare section of railing available. The drones flew back to the *Wilson*, but the captain decided to ditch them because the seas were too rough for a landing.

"*Andiamo*, this is Captain Peters on the *Wilson*. From what you said, Captain, you seem to be stable. We're heading toward you now and should be on station in a few minutes. Meanwhile the flotation gear will keep you upright."

Captain Peters of the *Wilson* looked at his first officer and said, "Remind me to buy stock in Robot Depot, the company where we got the drones. Those machines just saved a bunch of lives."

CHAPTER TWELVE

Carly dropped Jenny and me in front of the Delta terminal at JFK.

"Thanks, Carly," I said. "See you next week."

"It's my pleasure, Mike. Have a good time in Japan," Carly said as the porter loaded our luggage onto a cart. The passengers lined up on the sidewalk stared. It will take some time for people to adjust to conversations between machines and humans. In our house, it's second nature.

Jenny and I were off to Nagasaki, Japan, to visit the Henn na Hotel, the first hotel in the world fully run by robots. I was investigating robotic hotels as a possible new market for Robot Depot to explore, although Jenny had her doubts. I decided against taking the Gulf Stream because of the distance to Japan.

"I'm keeping an open mind, Mike, but it creeps me out to think that we'll be dealing with robots for our entire stay. Hotels are supposed to be friendly places, not machine driven. What's Henn na mean in English anyway?"

"It means 'strange' or 'weird,' " I said. Jenny just rolled her eyes.

"What does Blanche think about it?"

"You know Blanche," I said. "She thinks we should try new markets, even weird ones. Even in New York a hotel with the odd name Yotel employs a robot called a Yobot to help guests to store their luggage. The thing was manufactured by a competitor of ours in Connecticut. The Yotel also has self-service automated check-in kiosks. Blanche is going crazy over this, and wants to move us into the hotel market by next year."

The Henn na Hotel is located in Sasebo, in Nagasaki Prefecture in Japan. As we drove up to the place, I was impressed by its simple architecture, nothing fancy, just functional. The hotel is located on the top of a sloping lawn, a nice touch, I thought. Not exactly the Waldorf, but it was clean and neat. We walked into the lobby, and received our first shock.

"You've got to be kidding me, Mike. Tell me I'm not seeing that thing."

We walked up to the check-in desk and were greeted by a dinosaur wearing a bellman's cap—a dinosaur, or rather, an animatronic dinosaur that looked like a five-foot velociraptor if I recalled the name right from *Jurassic Park*. "He" greeted us in English.

"Welcome to the Henn na Hotel, folks," the dinosaur said. "I hope you enjoy your stay with us." The thing held out its claws in front of it, and the jaws moved as it spoke, as if it were chewing on tough steak. Its head also moved from side to side. The word "creepy" doesn't quite capture the essence of the experience.

"I've got a great idea, Mike. Why don't we sleep on a park bench tonight?"

"Hey, Jen, look at it as fun. When was the last time you were greeted in a hotel lobby by a dinosaur?"

"Actually, this is my first, and hopefully my last time," Jen said. "I think I'd prefer to deal with that nice looking lady next to the dinosaur."

"Look closely, Jen. She's a robot too."

The dinosaur then asked us to move to the right so our faces could be scanned. I thought this was a pretty ingenious type of room security. To get into your room all you had to do was place your face next to a screen. An orange cart then came wheeling up next to us. The dinosaur advised us to put our bags on the cart.

After the face-recognition window let us into our room, we noticed a little robot on the night table next to the bed. The bot can answer a variety of questions such as the time of day and the weather. Because of Jenny's talent with languages, we were able to wind our way through the array of Japanese speaking robots.

After we unpacked we went down to the lobby to ask the concierge about local places to eat. The robotic concierge looked like something from Toys"R"Us, but even though it looked like a toy, the thing was helpful with its programmed knowledge of local restaurants.

"Mike, we like to stay at high-end hotels. This place just doesn't do it for me."

"That's the whole idea, Jen. This place is neat and clean, but definitely not high-end. The idea of the robots running the place is pure economics. This is about 70 percent cheaper than a five-star hotel. Hell, it only cost us $80 per night. It may be creepy, but robots do save a lot of overhead. Think about a chain of budget hotels run by Robot Depot bots."

"Well, we're here for a market research and a learning experience, Mike, but after a couple of days let's get the hell out of here and go to the Four Seasons in Tokyo."

"The Four Seasons is a lovely hotel, madam, but I remind you that the Henn na Hotel is only $80 per night," the concierge said, apparently having overheard our conversation.

Jenny barked something in Japanese to the robot.

"Pardon me, madam, but I am not programmed to fuck myself."

CHAPTER THIRTEEN

As I promised Jenny, we spent our last two nights in Japan at the Four Seasons in Tokyo, waited on by a world class group of human beings. On the morning after we returned to Long Island, Jen and I were having breakfast at home when the phone rang. Omelet, our cooking bot, had prepared two delicious, well, omelets.

"Mike, it's Blanche on the phone," Jenny said. "She's upset about something. She told me to put it on speaker."

"Are you two watching News 12?"

"No," I said, "they giggle too much. We're watching Fox."

"Click it on now. They're about to run the segment again, and believe me it's nothing to giggle about. You've got a big day ahead of you, Mike. I'll meet you at your office. Put me on speaker while you watch the TV."

The camera panned on an attractive woman sitting on a park bench. A man, whom we recognized as Dennis Bliedner, a News 12 reporter, sat on the other end of the bench.

"Hello, my name is Dennis," Bliedner said to the woman.

"Hi Dennis, my name is Heather. You look lonely. Care for some company?"

"Holy shit," I said. "It's 7:30 in the morning. This looks a bit mature for kids who may be watching."

"It gets better—or worse," Blanche said. "Just keep watching."

"Why don't you sit next to me, handsome?" Heather said. "I'd like to get to know you."

Just then Bliedner stood, microphone in hand and his back to the lovely Heather.

"Friends, what you just saw is a phenomenon that is becoming more common in our modern age. The attractive lady behind me is not a lady at all but a robot. John Beekman, a man from Dix Hills, states that he met a beautiful woman in an encounter like the one you just witnessed. He and the woman married, but he soon discovered that she was not a woman, but, you guessed it, a robot. Humanoid robots are becoming frequent visitors to our communities. They can be purchased at retail outlets like Robot Depot right here on Long Island. Mr. Beekman says that the machine he thought was his wife began to malfunction. When he went to Robot Depot to complain he was treated discourteously, he claims, the clerk referring to his partner as a 'sex-bot.' Beekman says that he has been unable to sleep and suffers from emotional distress. He plans to sue Robot Depot. We'll be following this strange story and we'll bring you updates when we get them. This is Dennis Bliedner—and no, I'm not a robot—reporting for News 12, Long Island.

⛬

"May I please speak to James Brody? This is Philip Townsend, attorney for Robot Depot."

"Hi Phil, Jim Brody here. Something tells me you're calling about the antics of my former client, John Beekman."

"Your *former* client?" Townsend asked.

"Yes, former. We agreed that it would be best for all if he was represented by another lawyer."

"So I guess you don't want to say anything negative about your former client." Townsend said.

"That's right, Phil. The rules of ethics prevent me from telling you what a fucking lunatic he is. But you guys aren't out of the woods yet. Mr. Beekman has hired as my replacement, none other than Wally Yaeger."

"Wally Yaeger, Long Island's premier ambulance chaser?" Townsend said.

"He doesn't chase ambulances, Phil, he lies down in front of them."

"I suppose he's going to portray Robot Depot as a greedy predator," Brody said, "playing on the sexual hang-ups of shy people. If there's one thing that Yaeger loves more than money it's publicity. The story may have started here on Long Island, but Yaeger's PR people will have a segment in news reports across the country, maybe even the world. So Robot Depot will go from the highly respected business leader to the pimp on the corner selling sex-bots to horny assholes like my former client. If this case goes to trial, Phil, you'll see me sitting in the back of the courtroom with a bag of popcorn."

⚔

"I'm really not worried about this crap, Blanche," I said. "The simple fact is that we did not sell that robot to Beekman. He admits that he met the future 'Mrs. Beekman' in a bar. How the hell she got there is anybody's guess."

Phil Townsend and Jenny were in my office along with Blanche.

"I'm afraid that things are starting to get difficult, Mike," Townsend said. The three of us looked at him.

"Do you know something new, Phil?"

"Yeah, I have something new, and I wish I didn't. I've done a lot of investigating since we met that nut job Beekman. Here's what I found. Not only did we sell the bot, although not directly to Beekman, but we also manufactured the damn thing. As you know, we've been experimenting with female androids, figuring we could sell them as greeters, the same purpose as male robots. Hey, Mike, you and Jenny just showed us that video of that hotel in Japan. Remember that the desk clerk next to the dinosaur greeter was an attractive young woman—which happened to be a humanoid robot. I recently huddled with our defense counsel, a sharp bunch of people. They think that Yaeger the ambulance chaser wants to stretch the boundaries of product liability law and prove that we're liable for putting a sexually attractive bot into the stream of commerce, whether or not we sold it directly to that pervert Beekman."

"I've seen Yaeger at work, folks," Blanche said. "I once had a large client in the furniture business that Yaeger sued after his client caught her finger in a folding chair. It should have been a simple case with a settlement. Instead, Yaeger turned it into a crusade against my client, the evil predatory capitalist monster out to cripple the poor consumer. The company went from ten stores down to one, and that one is struggling."

"Mike," said the voice of Francine, my robotic receptionist, over the intercom, "*The New York Times* is on line two."

Blanche grabbed me by the hand. "Tell them you'll call back in 15 minutes. We need to come up with a standard response. You agree, Phil?"

"Yes, I agree," said Townsend, "but then we'll need to come up with a long narrative, not just some sound bites."

Francine told the *Times* that we'd call back.

"Another thing, Mike," Blanche said. "I think we need to take Francine off reception duty and replace her with a real person.

While I was waiting for you and Jenny, another newspaper reporter called, I think it was the *New York Post*. You weren't here to take the call or give Francine instructions, so she said to the reporter, and I quote, 'Fuck off, asshole. We didn't sell anything to that pervert from Dix Hills.' "

We all looked at Jenny.

"I think I better keep my mouth shut around our company bots."

CHAPTER FOURTEEN

Carly dropped me off at the rear entrance to the Robot Depot headquarters. I didn't want to wade through the crowd of about 30 picketers in front of the building. Although it was raining heavily, the picketers kept walking back and forth, waving their plastic signs. Not cardboard, but professionally printed waterproof signs. The words would be almost funny if I wasn't so angry.

"Robot Depot – Corporate Pimp"

"Robot Depot – Will your kids be the next target?"

"Robot Depot – The Giant of Automated Sleaze"

"Robot Depot – The Profits of Sin"

Blanche and Phil Townsend were waiting for me outside my office.

"Where's Jenny?" Blanche asked.

"She's manning our home phone. Somebody leaked our number."

"Mike, we have to act fast," Blanche said. "That scumbag Yaeger can arrange a demonstration in minutes. I recognize a lot of those faces on the picket line from other lawsuits that Yaeger's handled. He's one part lawyer, nine parts PR machine."

I laughed. "Who would believe that nonsense? It's obvious that it's a staged demonstration."

"It's obvious to us, Mike," Blanche said, "but on 24/7 TV news, it looks real. To a news producer, a soundbite is a soundbite, and he doesn't care who's paying the picketers."

"Blanche is right, Mike," Townsend said. "We need to get out in front of this bullshit as soon as we can. A few weeks from now it won't matter what the law is, or even the facts. The only thing that will matter is the picture that Yaeger can paint. He's brilliant at manufacturing perceptions."

"Any legal action yet, Phil?"

"We were served with the complaint first thing this morning. *John Beekman vs. Robot Depot and Michael Bateman.*"

"He named me in the complaint?" I said.

"I only read part of the caption, Mike. Jenny and Blanche are also defendants, along with almost every salesperson on your showroom floor. Yaeger's tactic is to cost so much money in legal fees that it becomes a lot cheaper to settle than to fight in court. His client's robot wife isn't the only one who's fucking people."

"I've lined you up to be interviewed by Shepard Smith on *Fox News* this afternoon," Blanche said. "He's got a reputation as a straight shooter, and also as a guy who doesn't put up with bullshit. It's a nationally syndicated show and it will buy us some time. His producers know how to put on an interesting show, so don't be surprised if you see a female android standing next to him."

I'm used to seeing Blanche remain calm under pressure, but as she spoke she was shredding a napkin.

"So what do I say to all the reporters calling, not to mention Shepard Smith?" I asked.

"Phil and I have been talking about just that question. Phil, tell Mike your radical idea."

"So here's my radical idea, as Blanche puts it," Townsend said. "Tell the truth, as simple and as radical as that. Tell them that Robot Depot has just recently gotten into the business of humanoid robots, and you're promoting them to be used as greeters and information providers. If people want to abuse a product, whether it's a robot or a barstool, Robot Depot can't control that."

"Easier said than done," I said. "I'm not a lawyer, Phil, but I know how it all works. This lawsuit is going to result in discovery, including written interrogatories and depositions. I'm sure that some of our younger marketing executives are on the record joking that we sell female androids for fun as well as business. Just a bunch of dumb ideas blurted out at marketing meetings, stupid jokes that sound like ideas, but ideas nonetheless—recorded ideas. Yaeger will probably put some of the quotes on the side of his car."

"One positive thing is this," Townsend said. "Although Yaeger always raises money and backers for his major lawsuits, it's nowhere close to the amount of cash that Robot Depot can throw at a case. We can squeeze his financial nuts until he yells."

"I wish I could be as optimistic as Phil," Blanche said. "Something tells me that Yaeger has some huge funding in the wings."

"Blanche is right, Phil. Yaeger is about to spring something on us."

CHAPTER FIFTEEN

"Good morning everybody, and what a beautiful morning it is—no shit," said one of our floor cleaning bots as he wheeled around the room. Obviously he'd been chatting with Jenny.

We were having a strategy meeting in my office with Blanche, Phil Townsend, and me. Jenny surprised us by showing up a half-hour after the meeting started.

"I thought you were going to monitor the telephone at home, hon"

"I decided to turn the phone off and get a new line."

"But what if it's a reporter with a deadline?" Blanche asked.

"Fuck 'em," Jenny explained.

"I hate to start the morning off with something negative, but I think we may have another problem," Blanche said. "On my way here this morning I remembered a TV interview that Mike did about two years ago on a Saturday morning business show. Eric Bolling, the host of *Cashin In*, asked Mike about the economic impact of robot technology. The show concentrated on robots that had business uses. They walked around our showroom

Robot Depot

floor, from bot to bot, from a hamburger making machine to a soda pourer, to a personal calculator, and on and on. Then Bolling hit Mike with the big question. I remember this like it was yesterday. 'On a per robot basis,' Bolling asked, 'how many employees do you think each of these machines replaces on average?' Without batting an eye, Mike, you said, 'Each of these robots replaces 10 employees.' If you recall, that show resulted in headlines and columns in newspapers and magazines over the following month."

"Oh, my God," Jenny said. "I think I see where you're going with this."

"You got it, Jenny," Blanche said. "We've got a union problem, a big fucking union problem. That's where Yaeger will get his funding for this lawsuit. From unions. They hate Robot Depot, and I'm guessing they'll invest tens if not hundreds of millions of dollars to bring Robot Depot to its knees. They see Robot Depot as a company dedicated to robbing hourly employees and entry level people by replacing their jobs with cheaper robots."

"But that's bullshit," I said. "Last year I wrote an article for the *Wall Street Journal* with Bill Gates. We both agreed that some kind of tax should be levied on job-taking robots for exactly that reason. I don't want to take jobs from people, but at the same time we can't stop technology from moving forward. We have to think it through and plan for the future."

"But the unions still hate you, Mike," Blanche said, "no matter how many op-ed pieces you write. They see you and Robot Depot as job stealers and that's that. Hell, I've read opinions by some union leaders over the years that even complained about the use of personal computers. They worry that spreadsheet software will displace armies of junior number crunchers."

Joe, the coffee making bot, came whirring up to the conference table with a pot of fresh-brewed coffee, performing a job that used to be held by a young assistant.

59

"On a positive note," Jenny said, "I think Mike did great on Shepard Smith's show yesterday. Smith didn't even have an android next to him."

"Yeah," I said, "but they did show a clip of an attractive female android, our Model 3510. The important thing is that he didn't show a hint of taking sides with John Beekman. Smith actually seemed like he was stifling laughter when we spoke about the guy. I think a lot of the big serious news shows will see the stupidity of this case, even the humor."

"It's a good thing hookers aren't unionized," Townsend said.

"Hey, here's an idea for a TV show," Jenny said. "*Celebrity Robot.*" At the end, instead of the host saying 'you're fired,' he says, 'you're unplugged.' "

"It's good we can laugh—while we're able to," Blanche said. "Tomorrow, Mike, the *60 Minutes* people will be here to tape your segment for next week's show. It will be the most important show you've ever done. Yaeger and his union backers will be watching intently."

CHAPTER SIXTEEN

"The American dream, boiled down to its essentials, is based on a simple premise," Lara Logan said at the start of a *60 Minutes* segment. "You get a job, work hard and you're on your way up the ladder. But the 'get a job' part of that scenario is becoming harder every day. It once meant that you would have to ride out a recession, but things would eventually turn around, and you'd be on your way. After the last recession, however, some economists and pundits are seeing something new on the labor horizon, automated labor; that's right, robots. Robotic labor has been used in manufacturing for years, but now it's become part of every segment of the economy. Entry level jobs often meant serving hamburgers. A staggering one in eight Americans once worked at MacDonald's, the fast food giant. What's wrong with slinging hamburgers as a first job? Nothing, absolutely nothing. It is, or was, a common first step up the ladder, a step where you learned the basics of having a job: Show up on time, work hard, and be friendly to customers. But robots can do the same job as an entry level kid. Robots don't get sick, always show up on time because they never leave, don't take vacations, don't drink or do drugs, and don't need health care or retirement benefits."

Logan paused to read the words on the teleprompter.

"And that's just fast food jobs. Robots are now being used as toll takers, store greeters, inventory counters, and floor cleaners, just to name a few job descriptions. Want to drive a cab until something better comes along? Soon, you'll be competing with driverless cars, which are basically robots on wheels. How about learning to be a writer? There is an enormous need for writers, including sports reporters and investment advisors. But all of those things I just mentioned now include robots in the picture.

"On a new TV show called *The Book*, a group of panelists were asked to discuss a book they were all assigned to read. Each one of them loved the book, the author's debut novel. Before the end of the show, however, the host dropped a bombshell. The 488-page novel, *Opening the Frontier*, was written by an artificial intelligence machine—a robot. And what about me and my colleagues on *60 Minutes?* We're all TV journalists. Will we be replaced by machines sometime in the future? I would have laughed at the idea not long ago, but after reading that robot-authored book, I'm not so sure. We're going to pause for a commercial break. I should tell you that all of the people you see in the commercials are real human beings. I think. When we come back we'll talk to a man who is at the center of this earth-changing movement."

After the break, the camera focused on a familiar floor-cleaning robot sucking up dust and dirt.

"Let me introduce you to Dusty, a room-cleaning robot," I said. "Hello Dusty, say hi to Lara and the viewers."

"Hello, everbody," Dusty said. "I love to watch *60 Minutes*, Lara. I check it out every Sunday at 7 p.m. Eastern Time while I'm doing the floor. Unless there's a football game, of course, but then I watch the show as recorded on my internal video recorder."

"We're here at ground zero of the robot revolution," Logan said, "and if you listened to Dusty, it seems like a friendly revolution indeed. Robot Depot is the megastore of the future, and quite a bit of the present as well. Michael Bateman, or Mike as he likes to be called, is the Bill Gates of robotics. He began with one store five years ago and is now in 30 states. He hopes to be in all states within three years. Mike Bateman is typical of the visionary entrepreneur. He saw a trend and got in front of it to lead the parade. But some see him as leading a parade of army tanks, blowing up or plowing down traditional institutions."

Lara Logan is a charming lady and an excellent reporter, but she talks so much I'm not sure they'll have any time for me.

"Mike, tell us about the future you see coming, a future that is being heavily influenced by Robot Depot."

"Lara, I see robotics and artificial intelligence as genies that recently popped out of a bottle. As much as some people may wish, the genies aren't going back in."

"But genies are in the business of granting wishes," Logan said. "Some people see you and your company as a way to take away wishes."

"You raise an important point, Lara, probably the most important point about robotics. Can machines take away simple jobs, entry level jobs? The answer is obviously yes, robots can do that. In your introduction to this segment you reviewed some of the major breakthroughs in AI and robotics. A novel written by a robot is a groundbreaking development."

"Do you know the person who invented that robot, Mike?"

"That's us. Angus the novel-writing robot is one of ours, invented and developed right here at Robot Depot headquarters."

I could tell by the look on Logan's face that she wanted to pummel her researcher for not alerting her to that.

"So what about the kid who can't get a job at MacDonald's because the job was taken by a robot?"

I could tell she wanted to get away from the subject of Angus as fast as possible.

"If you're asking whether it bothers me, Lara, the answer is yes," I said. "How much does it bother me? The answer is a lot. It bothers me enough to realize that we have to shift our thinking. Bill Gates is of the opinion that robots should be taxed to create a huge fund for displaced workers. I agree with him. You may be surprised to know that I'm a political conservative, but this issue has nothing to do with liberalism or conservatism. As a society, we need to ask ourselves the simple question: Are we willing to live with the idea of tens of millions of people displaced from work by machines? The answer is no, we don't want to live with that scenario and we've got to act responsibly. A country with a permanently unemployed cohort of people will quickly become a country of civil unrest. So I don't see the robot tax as a way to fund a new form of unemployment benefits, as attractive as that may sound to hordes of bureaucrats in Washington. No, I see it as a sort of alternate employment device.

"Take CBS for example, a company that employs a lot of people. Responsible managers only employ enough workers to fill a need. I bet there are a lot of managers at CBS, maybe you, who would love to hire more people, but know that to do so would be financially irresponsible. What if you had a huge fund to hire as many people as you want, not just who you need. Call it the Robot Fund or whatever. The point is that we can create new jobs as we close old ones. How insane would it be for a huge, successful company like Robot Depot to close down jobs and expect the taxpayer to pick up the difference with extended unemployment insurance?"

"On the subject of disappearing jobs, Mike, I understand that Robot Depot is investing in not only driverless cars but driverless trucks. Let's take a look at some upsetting facts. In the United States there are approximately 180,000 taxi drivers. On top of that number is the new car-for-hire on the block, Uber, and other driver-for-hire companies. We're told that Uber employs 600,000 people. Combine that with the number of traditional taxi drivers and we're looking at almost 800,000 people driving cars for employment. Then if we look at the trucking industry, we find that about 3.5 million people drive trucks for a living. What becomes of them when driverless trucks take over? And it gets scarier when you read about a service called Amazon Go, which was first announced at the end of 2016. Amazon has figured out how to automate supermarkets, using smart phone technology to eliminate checkout lines. When you eliminate checkout lines you eliminate checkout clerks. Supermarkets and the rest of the retail food industry employ about five million people, and Amazon is replacing them with technology, a lot of which was developed by Robot Depot.

"And speaking of Amazon," Logan continued, "how many jobs has that company alone added for the function of filling orders?—Picking stuff off a shelf and putting it into a box. The Wall Street Journal noted that American warehouses have added 262,000 jobs in the past five years just for that task. About 950,000 people are employed in warehouses filling online orders. Robot Depot is developing a class of robots that can perform the complex task of distinguishing between one product and another, carefully picking it up and placing it in a box. Add another group of people whose jobs will disappear forever. In the not so distant future, "picking" robots will replace all of those people. Oxford University did a study in 2014 and estimated that by 2034, 47 percent of all jobs will be automated. That's almost half of all jobs in just 20 years."

These *60 Minutes* people sure as hell did their research. But so did I.

"Again, Lara, you're bringing up shocking statistics of which I'm well aware. We can't ignore those statistics, because behind those numbers are real people who will be out of jobs in the near future. The economics can't be ignored. That's why I see a form of guaranteed employment as a development that will need to occur."

"Here's hoping that a visionary thinker like Mike Bateman keeps on being visionary," Logan said. "We'll see you next week, folks, assuming my job hasn't been taken by a robot. Thank you for watching *60 Minutes*. I'm Lara Logan signing off at Robot Depot."

Dusty, the floor cleaner, wheeled up to Lara Logan and said, "Nice job, Lara. I hope you come back again."

As I was taking out the earpiece, Lara walked up to me. "Mike, I interview a lot of people as you well know. I just want to tell you how impressed I am with you and your company. I thought this segment would be somewhat light and a bit controversial, but it turned out to be a lot more than that. You really are a visionary. I hope to book you again for a follow up segment, maybe to investigate what the stupid politicians will do to destroy your fantastic ideas."

As the CBS people packed up all their equipment I went to my office where Jenny and Blanche were waiting for me.

⊨⟨⊢ ⊣⟩⊨

"I want you to run for the senate, maybe the governorship, Mike," Blanche said. "And take me with you."

"Great job, honey," Jenny said. "Blanche is right. You'd make a great politician. After this *60 Minutes* segment, I think people will laugh at that robot-marrying asshole Beekman without our prompting them."

"Your lips to God's ears, Jenny," Blanche said. "But lawsuits assume a life of their own. Let's take it one day at a time. Hey, you two, enjoy a few days off. God knows you deserve it."

"We'll try, Blanche, "I said. "Billy Jackson, our resident genius, tells me he's made a groundbreaking discovery, and he's going to unwrap it at our vacation house."

"Wonderful," Blanche said. "We need a breakthrough."

CHAPTER SEVENTEEN

Carly drove Jenny and me to our lake house in the Adirondacks, our favorite place to get away when we want to do some heavy thinking and heavy relaxing. Our guest for two days would be the most secretive man at Robot Depot, Liam Jackson. We call him "Billy," after the 1982 movie, *Computers are People Too*, where a programmer gets transported into a computer. Billy is so bright it's almost creepy. I recruited him away from Cal Tech with the offer of a lot of money including profit-sharing, and most important, the ability to let his creative juices flow rather than bottle them up on the group-think campus of a modern university. Billy had once given a speech at Cal Tech on artificial intelligence and its implications for the future. He was picketed by 500 students and young faculty members who were against his philosophical musings. For reasons even the brilliant Billy couldn't figure out, he was labeled a fascist, racist, misogynist, and homophobe. In my first interview with him, Billy told me that the modern university sees anything new as a sinister right wing plot. He jumped at my offer, not so much for the excellent money, but for the freedom of being released from the mental bonds of academia. Billy is now our vice president in charge of science and research.

We expected him at 3 p.m., about four hours after our arrival. The late June weather was warm and dry, perfect for a week in the Adirondacks. I was lying down on a wide soft deck chair. Jenny came out with a tray of snacks and placed it on the table next to the chair. She then lay down on the chair next to me. She was totally nude.

"Hey, babe, not that I object, but we're expecting Billy."

"He won't be here for another few hours, plenty of time for us to get in some important exercise," she said as she undid the belt on my shorts. She reached down and held me. "Sometimes it's nice to get away from machines and enjoy the softer side of life," Jenny said as she moved her head downward. She looked up at me and said, "But not too soft."

We both fell asleep after a wonderful workout.

"Holy shit, I said, looking at my watch. "Billy will be here any minute."

"How quick?"

"Not too quick. Hell, Billy knows his way around here. He can let himself in."

When we got out of the shower our bathing assistant bot rolled up to us holding towels in its outstretched arms.

"I've warmed the towels for you, Jenny and Mike," said 'Sudsy,' the bot.

"Good grief, Sudsy, did you watch us?" Jenny asked.

"Yes, I saw everything. Quite instructive, but extremely confusing."

We went downstairs and I put on a pot of coffee. Billy loves coffee. The doorbell rang, and in walked Billy, wearing Hawaiian-style Bermuda shorts, a tie-died tee shirt, a white dinner jacket, brown loafers, and black knee socks. Billy never got the fashion memo.

As we sat down in the den for coffee, Sudsy came wheeling by to put the wet towels into the washing machine.

"You missed a great show, Billy," Sudsy said.

"Take a hike, Sudsy, we won't be needing your services anymore today," Jenny said, afraid that Sudsy would tell Billy all she learned about humans having sex.

"Hey, why don't we sit out on the deck," Billy said as he took a cigar out of his pocket. "It's a beautiful day." Besides coffee, Billy loves cigars.

"You guys know that I don't like to be dramatic, yes?"

"Yes," Jenny said. "You had a brilliant academic career, but I can't imagine you in the drama club."

Billy laughed and took a long pull on his cigar.

"Well, today I'm going to be dramatic. Today I'm going to show you the new future of Robot Depot." He paused. "Maybe even the new future of the world."

"What?" Jenny and I both said. Sometimes Billy's words come a lot slower than his thoughts.

"I've unlocked the secret to the world's first sentient robot."

Jenny and I said nothing. What we just heard sucked reality out of the air and let in science fiction. With all of the advancements in robotics and artificial intelligence over the years, almost all scientists agreed that a sentient machine is decades into the future, and a lot of them argued that it will never happen. Sentience, the ability of a being to be aware of itself, has always been the missing element in robot technology. Typical of Billy, he didn't share the majority view that a sentient robot was impossible. He just did his research and performed his experiments, expecting to one day sit down and have a chat with a robot. The day had come.

"You're being dramatic, Billy, and I think you know that," Jenny said. "Are you saying that you taught a bot to do a couple of thought experiment tricks and you're calling it sentience?"

"Why don't I let Angus speak for himself?"

"Angus?" We both said.

"Yes, named after Angus MacDougal, a Scotch physicist who I got most of the math from. But you're the boss, Mike, and you can name him whatever you want to. His real name is Model 48CV2."

"Hey, Billy, is Angus the same bot who wrote that novel everybody's talking about?" I asked.

"The one and only," Billy said. "Angus is working on his next novel."

"I've seen Angus in action working on the book writing contest we're doing with that TV show, *The Book*," I said, "but I had no idea that it was aware of itself, or I should say, '*he* was aware of *him*self. He's probably our most famous robot."

Billy then walked over to the edge of the deck and called down the driveway.

"Hey, Angus, come and join the meeting."

I felt like I was in the middle of a vivid dream, not a nightmare to be sure, but definitely a dream.

The rear doors of Billy's van opened and a bot with a walking mechanism stepped out. Billy had made no attempt to give the robot an android or human-like appearance. It was a robot without any doubt, with wires, gears, pulleys, and all the stuff that enables a bot to move. Angus walked over to the deck and climbed the steps perfectly. This was nothing new. We had developed walking and running bots with fluid movements plenty of times.

"Please sit down, Angus, it will make our friends more relaxed," Billy said.

Angus sat and moved its "head" toward me. I've been in the robot business for a long time, but this thing was giving me the creeps.

It, or he, began to speak. Because it had no lips to move, I again I noticed that Billy didn't make an effort to give Angus a human appearance.

"It's a pleasure to meet you personally, Mr. Bateman. Since you're the CEO of the company, should I call you boss or sir?"

"That won't be necessary, Angus, just call me Mike."

I'd been speaking to robots for many years, but this is the first time I spoke to a machine that understood what it was saying, not just mimicking human communication. I was starting to relax with our new friend.

"So tell us about yourself, Angus. By the way, I loved your book. And please call me Jenny."

"Well, Jenny, I've recently discovered who I am, thanks to Billy here. I understand that I've been in development for five years, and all of a sudden I had an epiphany?"

"Epiphany?" Jenny said, "You had a fucking epiphany? Robots don't have epiphanies."

"Billy warned me about your nasty language, Jenny, and he programmed me to avoid such words. But in answer to your question, yes, I've had a friggin epiphany. About three weeks ago I suddenly became aware of my existence. Billy installed a vision module, so I'm able to see. I looked at myself in a mirror and saw the jumble of tubes and wires that you're looking at. Billy tells me he's going to outfit me with android covering so I'll look more human."

"Angus, here's an important questions for you," I said. "How do you feel right now? Not how you think, but how do you *feel*, if you understand what I'm saying."

"I feel good, Mike, if I'm using the right word. I see that there's a fascinating world out there and I'm part of it. But one thing concerns me, Mike. You aren't going to sell me, are you?"

I'd just been struck speechless by a robot. This bot is concerned about his personal welfare, and just asked me pointedly about his future. It isn't rare for an employee to discuss his career with the boss, but this employee is not human. Is he even an employee? I wondered.

"Angus, I'm sorry for my delay in answering you," I said, "but you raise a question I never thought about before. Well, until meeting you this afternoon, I didn't have the ability to even form a question like that."

"The answer is no goddam way, Angus," Jenny said. "Mike is the boss, but I know him well enough that I know what he's thinking. My God, you have consciousness, sentience, self-awareness, things that we all thought were impossible. How the hell could we sell you to somebody else and be able to sleep at night? I mean—holy shit, you're a person."

I could swear that I saw Angus' steel shoulders drop a bit, as if he just heard something he felt relieved about.

"Angus and I discussed this subject, guys," Billy said. "I explained that Robot Depot is in the business of selling stuff. Don't worry, I inserted an economics module, so Angus knows all about business. But Angus' very existence changes the game, doesn't it? I agree with Jenny, Mike. How the hell can we sell a being that's self-aware?"

"Well, here's my answer," I said, "and I don't need to discuss it with the board. We're not going to sell Angus. From this point on, I will think of Angus as part of our management team."

"God bless you, Mike," Angus said. I couldn't believe that this robot just invoked the name of God.

"From everything I've heard about you," Angus continued, "I knew that you're a man of high ethics and morals. Yes, I know all about ethics, and right versus wrong. Billy has given me quite an education."

"Hey, dinner will be served shortly," Jenny said. "Our kitchen bot—we call her Kitchy—has prepared brisket of beef with all the trimmings. Angus, can I get you some old electric parts, maybe some used batteries." Jenny loves to play the wiseass, whether with human beings or robots.

We heard a strange sound, sort of like an old car horn, and then realized that it was Angus laughing at Jenny's dumb joke. This thing, or person, whatever, even has a sense of humor.

"Angus has some interesting ideas about the future of Robot Depot," Billy said. "Let's continue this conversation after dinner. I brought some nice wine."

"I'll just have a glass of battery acid," Angus said, laughing hysterically at his own joke. "ayooga, ayooga, ayooga."

We've got to do something about that laugh, I thought. He sounds like a Model T that's run out of oil. As hungry as I was I couldn't wait for dinner to be over so Angus could tell us about his ideas.

CHAPTER EIGHTEEN

After dinner, with the late June sun still high in the sky, we returned to the table on the deck. Jenny and I are used to being surrounded by robots with names, but we always knew that they were just programmed machines, and our "conversations" were the result of computer algorithms. Angus brought a new dimension to our lives, not to mention to the life of Robot Depot. Well, maybe even the world.

"Billy told me about your legal problems concerning that sexual robot, I believe you call it a sex-bot," Angus said, his "gaze" focused on me.

"It's a gigantic distraction, Angus, but I'm not worried about it."

"I can't agree with your sanguinity, Mike," Angus said. Billy gave him quite a vocabulary.

"I have spent a good amount of time on the Internet researching the attorney named Wally Yaeger. I then ran statistics on the cases he's tried. Yaeger is the most winning trial lawyer in the country, succeeding at 96 percent of the cases he handles. According to his peers, Yaeger has an uncanny ability to spot a winning set of facts and make millions with it. It's easy to dismiss the idea of a lonely man being seduced by a robot. I have watched late night comedy shows, and it appears that this lawsuit is one of the greatest things that ever happened to joke writers. But, I repeat, do not underestimate attorney Yaeger. I have seen photographs of the female android who attracted the attentions of the plaintiff, and she conforms to what I've learned is human female beauty."

"Would you take her out on a date, Angus?" Jenny asked, at her embarrassing best.

"Well, Jenny, if Billy had programmed me to be sexually active, I would consider that lovely android a 'fox;' not as sexy as you, but attractive nonetheless."

I couldn't wait to talk to Jenny later about how she felt being flirted with by a robot.

"Any thoughts on what we can do about this crazy lawsuit, Angus?" I asked

"Billy told me about your consultant and PR person Blanche. I've researched her and I advise you that she is the best we can have on our side."

"I notice that you said *our* side, Angus. Do you feel like you're one of us?"

"Yes, I do. You are my friend."

"What's next, Angus?" Jenny asked. "Can you recommend steps we should take?"

"Yes, Jen. Because Billy invented a way for me to process information far beyond what any artificial intelligence machine has ever done, I can make constant recommendations. I can even make predictions based on trends that I see."

"Can you tell us about a trend we haven't spotted yet?" Billy asked.

"Yes, negative journalism for one thing. Robot Depot used to be popular with journalists both in print and live media. Reporters find a never-ending source of interesting news from Robot Depot activities. The most recent source of news is the *Beekman* lawsuit about the sexbot. I have calculated that all of the major networks have devoted eight percent of print or airtime to that story alone over the past two weeks."

"So what's the big trend, Angus?" I asked "We've known for a long time that the media finds us interesting and gives us constant free publicity."

Angus swiveled his head toward me abruptly. I had the weird feeling he was about to call me a jerk for not spotting what he had seen.

"Here is the trend, Mike. Robot Depot was once a source of interesting news, but now it's emerged into a source of scandalous news. The media loves villains, people they don't trust. It enables them to compete with TV scripts where there's a new bad guy every week. I see the media turning on Robot Depot now. It started with the *Beekman case.* Your appearance on *60 Minutes* with the reporter Lara Logan was excellent, but that was yesterday. The story line now is the big greedy corporation taking advantage of a poor vulnerable man and ruining his life—all in the name of profits. The media wants to make Robot Depot synonymous with greed."

"But how the hell can they do that?" Jenny asked, her voice tinged with exasperation. "Just because one asshole falls in love with a robot hardly makes Robot Depot greedy. How can they portray us as a force of evil?"

"We will prove them wrong, Jen. We will show them the positive influence Robot Depot brings to the world. Billy, have you told Jenny and Mike about Columbia Presbyterian?"

Jen and I looked at Billy. Neither of us had heard anything about Columbia Presbyterian. "Obviously I haven't confirmed any plans yet without clearing them through you," Billy said, "but I think you're going to love what you're about to hear. I had lunch a few weeks ago with Doctor Brian Fuller, the medical director of Columbia Presbyterian Medical Center in Manhattan. He's a big fan of artificial intelligence and its uses in medicine. Angus and I have created a gigantic medical database module called Robot Diagnostics. To be a bit dramatic, let me say that it will revolutionize medicine the way Angus has revolutionized novel writing. With your okay, Mike, I'll set up a demonstration of Angus' capabilities in front of Dr. Fuller and a staff of physicians."

Maybe we should change the name of the company to Angus, Inc., I thought. We were about to revolutionize of how medicine is practiced.

CHAPTER NINETEEN

Columbia Presbyterian is shorthand for New York Presbyterian-Columbia University Medical Center, one of the world's best hospitals, and a training ground for physicians. Dr. Brian Fuller, the medical director, is a visionary thinker. I couldn't be happier with Billy's choice of research hospitals.

Billy had laid the groundwork for our meeting, but I figured it was appropriate that I call the doctor myself. If this plays out it will be a major benchmark in the history of Robot Depot.

"Dr. Fuller, a Mr. Mike Bateman is on line three for you. Isn't he the robot guy?"

"Yes, Jesse, he's definitely the robot guy. We're shopping for a robot to replace you."

"That's line three, wiseass."

Fuller is well known as an informal guy who's loved by his subordinates. He's as down to earth as a world famous genius can be.

"Doctor Fuller here, please call me Brian. Are you Mike Bateman?"

"Yes, Brian, and please call me Mike."

"I've had some long chats with your chief scientist Billy Jackson. It's always fun to talk to a true genius. Billy blew my fucking mind, Mike, please pardon my medical terminology. You guys at Robot Depot are way ahead of the curve in medical AI. As he may have told you, I've advocated the use of AI in medicine for so long I think that I started with the first robot. He told me all about Angus, the first robot in history that actually shows signs of sentience, an absolute breakthrough. But I'm really interested in the diagnostic database that Billy Jackson and the thing put together."

"Angus prefers to be referred to as a person," Brian. "He'll get pissed off if you refer to him as 'the thing.' "

"Far be it for me to piss off a robot," Fuller said, laughing. "So we're on for next Thursday. I'll have a group of about 150 doctors there for the demonstration. I hope one of them is a urologist because I just may pee in my pants."

⚊┆╌┆⚊

Carly drove Jenny and me to the office, where we met Billy and Angus. Billy folded up Angus, placed him into a carrying case, and set him down in the trunk. He didn't see any problem with the arrangement, because Billy had told him that bots often ride in the trunk. Angus kept busy by striking up a conversation with Carly. We could hear their muffled chatting on the speaker in the trunk.

Carly drove us to the rear entrance of the hospital on West 168th Street. An aide greeted us at the door and placed Angus' trunk onto a gurney. "Thank you," Angus said, scaring the shit out of the young aide. He took us to the auditorium, where most of doctors had already assembled. We sat at a table on the platform.

Dr. Brian Fuller was at the microphone and introduced us, including Angus whom he referred to as "that handsome pile of pipes over there." Angus found this quite funny and laughed hysterically—"ayooga, ayooga, ayooga." Billy leaned over to me and said softly, "I know, I know, I've got to fix the laugh."

"Ladies and gentlemen," said Dr. Fuller, "you know that I'm not an overly dramatic guy—well, maybe sometimes. But what you will hear and see today is a dramatic breakthrough, a dramatic advance in science, and a dramatic new page in the history of medicine."

"This guy's good," Jenny whispered to me. "Blanche would love him."

"Everybody in the audience, as well as me, shares something in common," Fuller continued. "We're all medical professionals. Boiled down to its essence, what we do is help people with their illnesses and sometimes cure them. So let me pose a question to the audience. Just shout out your response. Here's the question: How does the healing process start?"

"Diagnosis," almost everyone in the audience said. A few said "proper diagnosis," others "accurate diagnosis." Fuller smiled.

So at least everybody knows what they're supposed to do, I thought. Now let's see how good they are at doing it. The fun was about to begin.

"Here's how this presentation will work," Fuller said. "Everyone will be handed a sheet with symptoms, along with details on the patient, including prior incidents, surgeries, family history, and so forth. You will also receive the result of recent physical tests such as blood work, urinalysis, and any radiological tests such as a CT scan. These are actual cases. Our friend Angus will be given the same sheet that you're given. Yes, he's able to read. I don't want to embarrass anybody—that's not the purpose of this presentation—so therefore you won't be called on to deliver your diagnosis; it will be strictly voluntary. Please don't start to read until you're given the okay. Until I give you the go ahead, please keep the questions face down. You will be given a maximum of 10 minutes to read the information sheet. If you want to answer, just press the button on the arm of your chair. You can give a diagnosis for as many cases as you chose. Except for Angus that is. He'll give a diagnosis for *every* case."

The first item involved a 65-year-old male who complains of constant fatigue as well as occasional muscle pain and a bunch of other lesser symptoms. Fuller gave the signal, and everybody read about the guy's complete history. The buzzer sounded.

"Yes, Doctor Gillespie, your diagnosis, please."

"The gentleman in question suffers from macrocytic anemia, an insufficient amount of hemoglobin. I recommend vitamin and dietary therapy with a concentration on additional intake of iron."

A bunch of heads nodded in agreement.

"Ayooga, ayooga, ayooga," came the laugh from Angus. I gave Billy Jackson a look that advised him that his sudden death is imminent if he doesn't fix that fucking laugh. We're here to show people that Angus is a better diagnostician than them, but not to laugh at their mistakes. Thank God, Brian Fuller had a sense of humor.

"Well, it sounds like Angus doesn't quite agree with the consensus diagnosis. May I ask Angus to please vocalize his diagnosis?"

"Yes, the man does suffer from macrocytic anemia," Angus said, "but it's secondary to cancer of the colon which metastasized to the liver. I recommend immediate chemotherapy for one month. If the tumors have not shrunk appreciably after one month, I recommend surgery to excise them. Shortly after surgery, I recommend a CT scan to see if any cancer cells may have migrated to the lymph nodes, in which case I will recommend continuing with chemotherapy."

"Well, folks, Angus nailed it. Yes, metastatic cancer was the cause of the anemia. My assistants are now passing out the next case."

After a brief lunch break, the day continued. By four in the afternoon, the group had reviewed the records of 17 patients. Angus correctly diagnosed all of them, including three cases where nobody else had a clue.

"You all know that I'm a nut for statistics," Dr. Fuller said, "so I decided to run some stats on today's presentation. I timed how long it took from when you were told to read the symptoms and the sound of the first buzzer. The average time was eight minutes, thirty seconds, which I think is pretty impressive. But I also kept stats on the time it took Angus to press the button. Take a deep breath folks. It took Angus 15 seconds to read the symptoms and render a diagnosis. So, that's eight-and-a-half-minutes for the humans among us, and 15 seconds for the robot. And here's another shocker, my friends. Remember, I told you that all of the cases we looked at were real. The only thing that changed was the name of the patient. I hate to say this, but of the 17 cases we studied, five of the patients died—as a result of an incorrect diagnosis." He let his words sink in.

"Folks, Robot Depot has made medical history today."

We all piled into Carly for the trip back to Long Island.

"Mike, if that presentation today proved one thing, it's that Robot Depot is a force for good," Jenny said. "You heard what Dr. Fuller said at the end of the meeting. Five of the seventeen cases resulted in death as a result of a faulty diagnosis. If Angus was on the job, they all would have lived. My God, Mike—Robot Depot has just rewritten medical history. Do you think the media will give a shit, or do you think they'll remain fascinated by John Beekman, the robot-marrying pervert?"

"The media will go the path of least resistance," I said, "which usually means they look for bad news. It's something we just have to live with."

"I can't wait to hear your commencement speech at NYU next week, honey. I think a university crowd will love the news about Angus and the diagnostic results."

"A university crowd?" Billy Jackson said. "Be prepared to duck."

CHAPTER TWENTY

Most college commencements are held in June. What clown ever came up with the idea of wearing black robes in the sweltering heat? Jenny and Blanche sat near the podium where I was about to deliver my speech. Both of them had a lot of input into writing the speech, which made me a little intimidated that one of them would shout out that I missed a sentence.

The president of NYU had just introduced me as I walked up to the microphone.

"Good aftern..." I started to say. I started, but that's as far as I got.

"Fascist job-killing homophobic racist motherfucker," intoned one of the young scholars.

"Capitalist pimp," suggested another.

"Don't kill another job, kill yourself, scumbag," screamed a pretty coed.

"Racist, misogynist, fascist, rapist, capitalist..." shouted a student who suddenly ran out of "ists."

"Hey hey, ho ho—Robot Depot's got to go," Began the chant

"Hey hey, ho ho—Robot Depot's got to go."

"Hey hey, ho ho—Robot Depot's got to go."

The background music for all of the epithets hurled my way was, of course, "Hey hey, ho ho—Robot Depot's Got to Go." At least it rhymed. Maybe the words were written by a poetry major.

Apparently not satisfied with screaming, one of the young intellectuals jumped onto the platform and raced at me with his sign over his head. No doubt he hadn't gotten the memo that I'm a Marine combat veteran. I grabbed the stick, stepped lightly to the side, and used his oncoming force to pitch him off the stage face first into the ground. I looked to see Jenny and Blanche, who were surrounded by cops. I heard the crowd screaming—no surprise there. But after a couple of moments I realized the screaming was more of a cheer, and they were cheering for me. From what people later told me, when I flipped the young asshole to the ground, the crowd abruptly turned in my favor. I think they were with me to begin with, but they just shut up in the face of the marauding scholars. That's how riotous demonstrations work. People get scared and intimidated. But within minutes the crowd was no longer daunted by the loud radicals and decided on a counter-demonstration. I almost laughed when I scanned the audience and realized that the normal people outnumbered the protesters by more than double. So the festivities went from a demonstration to a riot to a bunch of brainless kids getting the shit kicked out of them. The cops seemed to enjoy seeing the radicals being stomped, judging from their slow response to the violence.

The lefties appeared to be frightened. I could see them scattering, their signs left behind on the grass. They were limping, bleeding, and in some cases crying. One hulking young idiot decided to keep the fun going. He stood on a chair and began to shout one of the approved debate slogans, "You fascist, racist, motherf..." His proclamation was suddenly interrupted by a fist to his stomach, followed by four punches to his face, all delivered by a tall man wearing an expensive suit. It was hard to believe but things actually started to calm down. Score one for Western civilization, I thought.

"Speech, speech, speech," the crowd chanted. Imagine that. A crowd of people chanting that they wanted to hear a message, not squelch it.

Jenny and Blanche came up to the dais.

"They want to hear you, honey. Don't disappoint them," Jenny said.

I noticed a bandage on Blanche's hand.

"What happened?"

"You didn't see it? Blanche clocked one of the assholes, but cut her hand on his sign."

"I'm dying to hear your speech, Mike, especially since the idiot protestors have calmed down," Blanche said.

I approached the microphone when Professor Brad Bartholomew, president of NYU, approached me.

"I'm concerned that alternative viewpoints may not be represented after the events of this afternoon," Bartholomew said. "How about skipping your speech, Mr. Bateman?"

"How about I break your fucking nose," I said, my patience having completely abandoned me. "If you want me out of here, you'll have to arrest me."

He let me speak.

I spoke.

The crowd, including a few students, went wild. They seemed to love the part about how the country can prepare for the inevitable job losses, and the details I gave for just how to do it. Then I discussed Angus, our artificial intelligence robot, with its medical diagnostic database, and how it would revolutionize medicine and save lives. That got a standing ovation. I also spoke about the TV show *The Book*, and how Angus the robot wrote a best-selling novel. I realized that the subject of computer-written novels could be controversial, so I pointed out the benefits of AI to the literary community and I invited anyone who may be interested to compete in the *Write the Book* competition, which would begin next month with us as a sponsor.

NYU President Bartholomew sat in the first row during my talk, looking troubled. He was no doubt wondering how he could explain the fact that a crypto-fascist microagressor like me was even invited to speak to the inquiring minds who would no doubt occupy his office tomorrow.

CHAPTER TWENTY-ONE

"You realize that Robot Depot has gone through a transformation, Mike, don't you?" Jenny said, as we had breakfast in our garden room, served by Omelet, our cooking bot.

I knew she was right, but I wanted to hear her thoughts on the subject.

"I think you're right, Jen, but tell me why you think that's so."

"Mike, we've gone from a successful company that sells tons of its products, to a company that's transforming the way life happens. We're now up there with Microsoft, Apple, and Google. We not only sell a lot of stuff, we're making a gigantic difference in the world. From medical technology, to life saving drones, to novel-writing robots, we're making people's lives better. And it's all because of you, handsome."

"It's not all because of me. If it weren't for you, I couldn't have come up with half the things we've pulled off, but thank you for saying that. I agree, Robot Depot has gone through a transformation recently, in spite of that robot-marrying idiot who's suing us. Things have never looked better."

Sometimes Jen and I just like to sit and enjoy our conversation. The subject couldn't have been more pleasant—Robot Depot making a huge positive difference in the world. For the first time in weeks I felt calm and relaxed.

"Hey, what the hell is this?" Jenny gasped as she set her cup down hard, splashing coffee onto the table. She turned the newspaper toward me. "How can a floor cleaner explode?"

The headline read. "Robotic Floor Cleaner Explodes, Burning Down a House in Suburban Los Angeles, Killing Two." The article went on to explain that the battery in the device was known to overheat, and that the machine came from Robot Depot.

The phone rang. It was Phil Townsend. I put him on speaker.

"This is a hit job, Mike," Townsend said. "This goddam fire happened last night. How the hell can anybody find the supposedly burned-out robot, arrange for it to be examined by experts, and come to a conclusion that it's ours?"

"And it's only 7:45 in the morning," I said. "That's 4:45 a.m. LA time."

While Phil was on the phone, Jenny was channel surfing on the TV, looking for other news reports.

"Listen to this, guys," Jenny yelled. She paused the broadcast and hit play when she got our attention.

"Randy Malcolm reporting from WABC. Last night was a night of horror for many families across the nation. No fewer than five floor cleaning robots manufactured and sold by Robot Depot have overheated and exploded during the night, causing three houses to burn to the ground and resulting in 10 deaths, including four children. We called Robot Depot home office on Long Island to ask for an explanation and were told "No Comment.""

"Bullshit," Townsend said. "I've been here since seven and nobody has called, and there were no messages. Obviously a call like that would go to Mike's office or to me as chief legal counsel. Somebody's fucking with us, big time."

"We're going to the office now, Phil. Please call Blanche and ask her to be there. Also, call Billy Jackson. I want input from him and Angus on this one."

Carly dropped us off at the main entrance. The latest group of picketers were sipping coffee, warming up for their day of chanting. They were much calmer than the group at NYU the other day, but of course the people picketing the office didn't give a shit because they were paid protesters. It was a beautiful late June day, with low humidity and not a cloud in the sky. Jenny and I had planned to take a day off and go sailing, but the national news media had other ideas.

We walked into the main lobby and were welcomed by our friendly greeter bot, Dick.

"Good morning, Mike, good morning, Jenny" Dick said.

"What's so fucking good about it?" Jenny inquired.

"The sun is shining and there isn't a cloud in the sky," said the always positive Dick.

We walked into my office. Waiting in the ante-room were Phil Townsend, Blanche, Billy Jackson, and Angus. Billy had been working on various android outfits for Angus to keep him from freaking people out. That day he wore a head that looked human, right down to facial tics and lips that formed words like a human being. Blanche had been introduced to Angus the day before and was developing a marketing plan to capitalize on our new groundbreaking robot.

I called Jack Winston, our engineer in charge of quality control, and asked him to join the meeting.

As Blanche had suggested, we replaced Francine, our robot receptionist, with a human being, a sharp woman named Dianne Knight from our marketing department. Dianne knew how to handle difficult calls, and that morning all of the calls were difficult. Unlike Francine, the receptionist robot with an attitude, Dianne never told a reporter to go fuck himself.

"Okay," I said, "I have the same question as everyone else. What the hell is going on? Jack, what's the word from quality control?"

Jack Winston is one of our best executives. He's an electrical engineer in charge of one of our most critical departments—quality control.

"I got my first call at five this morning and came right here," Winston said. "All seven of my people are pulling apart every floor cleaning bot to check on the batteries."

"Call your people off, right now, Jack. I don't want anybody hurt if those machines are explosive. Tell me about the batteries."

"As we all know," Winston said, "we got rid of the original batteries because they *did* pose a fire risk. We had sold only a handful before we decided to replace the batteries, even though the risk was slight. We replaced every one of them with a Marcus 3490 battery, the most reliable battery on the market. They're so safe that the Secret Service requires any robotic device used at the White House to include only a Marcus 3490. We give up a slight bit of battery life for a lot of safety. We don't even have any of the old Gentry 38 batteries on site. We dumped them all."

"Have we been contacted by any police or fire departments about the exploding machines?" I asked.

"Here's where the story gets totally weird," Winston said. "I didn't receive one call from any emergency responder. So I called the local police and fire departments in the areas where each of the explosions occurred. Each of them told me the exact same story—that they have the wreckage of each machine, but not one has been examined yet. *Not one.*"

"Then how the hell did the press get the idea that these were our machines?" I looked at Angus.

"Sabotage," Angus said. "It's the only possible conclusion from the data that we have."

"Wait a minute," Jenny said. "We don't just sell directly to the consumer; we market our stuff through retail outlets all over the country. Last night's fires occurred in three different states, one of which was California. If a machine leaves here with a good battery, a Marcus 3490, can we believe that somebody sabotaged the machines in three different states over God knows how many retail outlets. Angus, can you analyze what I just said."

Angus looked around from face to face, a slight whirring sound coming from his neck area.

"The inescapable conclusion is that the sabotage was done, and is being done, by an insider. Someone at our manufacturing facility is either replacing the Marcus 3490 batteries with exploding batteries, or simply inserting an explosive device having nothing to do with batteries." "You mean like a time bomb?" Jenny asked.

"Yes, a time bomb, or a device that can be detonated by a remote instrument."

"I've got to call the FBI," I said.

⇥ ⇤

"May I please speak to agent Rick Bellamy."

Rick is in charge of the New York Office of the Counterterrorism Task Force. I didn't think our problem had anything to do with terrorism, but Rick is an old friend, and I knew he'd point me in the right direction. Rick and I have been good friends for years. We grew up in the same neighborhood in Oyster Bay and went to the same elementary and high school. As an FBI man, Rick is a straight up and down guy. "I go where the evidence leads me," he often says, usually while being interviewed on TV about a case he just cracked.

"Hello, Mike, you've saved me a dime. I was about to call you. I guess we both want to talk about the same topic, last night's fires. This is a secure line, so feel free to talk."

"Here's what I know, Rick. All five of the suspected robotic floor cleaners are in police or fire department custody, and not one has been examined or inspected by an expert. But the media is treating this as a simple case of Robot Depot selling dangerous machines. Hell, we don't even know if they're Robot Depot products. But if they are, we're convinced that it was an inside sabotage job. If those machines are ours, and they probably are because we've almost cornered the market on devices like that, then the footprints lead directly to our manufacturing plant. I'm not even thinking about the legal issues—I just want the bombings to stop."

"You're a good man, Mike, and this phone call proves it," Bellamy said. "Yes, I believe you're right that it was an inside job. No way could somebody place bombs in machines sold through as many as five different outlets in three different states. So here's what I'm thinking. Somebody's out to fuck you and your company. The question is why. When five bombs go off in three different states, I get a whiff of terror, which is my job. Your manufacturing plant is in Hempstead, is that right?"

"Yes. It doesn't surprise me that you're on top of the case already."

"I'll meet you there in two hours," Bellamy said. "I don't want too many people at our meeting. Let's keep this small for the time being."

"I'll bring Phil Townsend, our legal counsel, and Jenny, who you haven't seen in a while. I suggest that I bring a guy named Jack Winston, our quality control vice president."

"No, Mike, don't bring Winston. As of right now he's a person of interest. For now, just bring Jenny and Townsend."

I was glad the phone wasn't on speaker so Jack Winston didn't hear Bellamy's thoughts about him being a person of interest.

Phil Townsend took his own car because he lived in Garden City, near our plant in Hempstead.

As Carly drove us to meet Rick Bellamy, Jenny grabbed my hand.

"We started our day talking about the wonderful transformation of Robot Depot into a world-changing force for good," Jenny said. "I think your FBI friend is right. Somebody's out to fuck us."

CHAPTER TWENTY-TWO

On a warm Wednesday morning, Chuck Walsh, general manager of the Jameston Building in Chicago, surveyed his recent purchases with his assistant, Nancy Fleming.

"My father was a union man," Walsh said. "My grandfather was a union man. And I started out after college as a union guy too. Hey, I've got nothing against unions, and I definitely have no problem with workers, but when technology makes it so much cheaper to run things, you gotta take notice. Look at this place, Nancy, the second tallest building in the world, and I've saved a fortune just by automating routine tasks. On every floor we have a robotic vacuum cleaner, a plumbing tester, and an energy monitor, one of our best robots. The little thing just wheels around from floor to floor monitoring our heat and electricity usage. And what about the security desk? Instead of a high-paid employee monitoring all of the security cameras, we have a robot that can spot problems and call the guards. I wouldn't be surprised to see the guards replaced by machines in the future."

"All together we own 360 robots," Nancy Fleming said. "I have to admit, Chuck, you're making a believer out of me. In just one month we've saved over $130,000 just by using these machines."

"And just take a look at your iPad, Nancy. A simple app shows the location of every one of the bots, not that I suspect a machine may be goofing off. Another nice thing about these bots is that they don't take lunch, don't take coffee breaks, don't step outside for a smoke, don't join unions, and they don't break my balls if they have a gripe. That's because robots don't have gripes. Open the robot app on your iPad go to 'locations,' and tap 'all,' and you get a glimpse of where all of the robots are at any given time."

"Hey Chuck, this is weird. According to the app, all 360 robots are congregating on the 65th floor, like they're having a robot convention. I just don't get it. Each robot is programmed for random movements, except for the security desk. How the hell can they all go to the same location at the same time? Somebody's obviously feeding them new commands."

"What's on the 65th floor, Nance? Isn't that where we store cleaning fluids and stuff like that?"

"Yes, it is and I've been meaning to talk to you about that. Those cleaning materials are combustible as hell. I'm just not comfortable having all of that flammable crap concentrated on one floor. I think we should spread them out, don't you?"

"Well, the robots are designed to minimize static electricity, Nance, so we don't have to worry about a spark."

"Okay, let's not worry about a spark. But we're still left with the question of what the fuck all those robots are doing in the same place, please pardon my language. You just commented that robots don't join unions, but it sure as hell looks like they're having a union meeting on the 65th floor. How can they randomly wind up on the same floor? Chuck, it just doesn't make sense."

"What the hell was that?" Walsh yelled, looking upward.

"Sounded to me like an explosion," Nancy said. "Holy shit, look out the window."

They saw what appeared to be a sudden storm outside the building. Large pieces of furniture came crashing to the ground, along with a blizzard of paper and assorted debris.

"Oh dear God, Chuck. Tell me I'm not seeing that. Those are bodies I see falling and they're all smoking. Some of them are on fire."

"Let's look at the security monitor. Where the hell is the security monitor robot?"

"My guess is that he joined his colleagues on the 65th floor,"

They looked at the monitor which simultaneously shows 12 floors, one on each of the screens. Nancy sat at the desk and hit buttons to show different floors. In front of them was a scene of sickening chaos, and the closer to floor 65 the worse was the mayhem. Although they couldn't hear them, they could see that people were screaming.

"Pan to floor 65," Walsh said. All they saw was darkness. Apparently the security cameras on the 65th floor were destroyed.

Nancy kept saying "oh my God," as she looked out the window and saw the falling bodies.

"Stop looking out the windows, Nance. We've got work to do."

Walsh took out a key and opened a cabinet under the security desk. He put in a code and an announcement came over the PA system throughout the building.

"There is a fire in the building," came the recorded voice over the speakers. "Please find the nearest stairwell and walk down. Do not use the elevators. This is not a drill. I repeat, this is not a drill. Please remain calm and walk down the stairs."

They heard the sounds of fire engines pulling up to the building. Walsh saw a body fall on top of one of the fire trucks.

The fire chief walked into the building and Walsh almost tripped as he ran to meet him.

"I'm Chuck Walsh, the building manager. The explosion happened on the 65th floor where a lot of combustible cleaning materials are kept. Remember what happened to those firemen on 9/11. Please don't send any of your guys up there."

"Anything out of the ordinary just before the explosion?" asked the fire chief.

"All of the building's robots congregated on the 65th floor. We have no idea how or why."

⋙ ⋘

"Wolf Blitzer for CNN ladies and gentlemen, with an update on the tragedy at the Jameston Building in Chicago. The 130-floor building has collapsed and fallen to the ground, two hours after an explosion on an upper floor. Just as we saw on the morning of 9/11/2001, a mighty structure obeyed the laws of gravity and collapsed into a mountain of smoking rubble. At 2,690 feet tall, the Jameston Building was the second tallest building in the world, second only to the Burj Khalifa in Dubai. We've found out that an explosion occurred on the 65th floor of the building, a place where flammable cleaning materials were stored. One strange fact that we're not able to piece together is that all of the building's robotic machines congregated on that floor. The machines are programmed for random movements such as floor and window cleaning. Nobody has been able to tell us how all 360 of the building's robots wound up on one floor at the same time. The Jameston Building management had recently decided to go all robotic, and purchased the robots just a month ago from the manufacturing and retail giant, Robot Depot."

CHAPTER TWENTY-THREE

Jenny, Phil Townsend, and I were sitting in the conference room at our manufacturing facility in Hempstead, waiting for Rick Bellamy and his FBI group. Like most of the country, if not the world, we were watching the Jameston Building disaster on TV. I assumed that Rick Bellamy would be heading to Chicago to work on the gigantic case that just happened, but he said that he wanted to see me as arranged.

Just like the World Trade Center, the Jameston Building collapsed after two hours. The camera left the scene of destruction for a few moments, and CNN anchorman Wolf Blitzer appeared on the screen. We had just achieved one of our greatest marketing coups by outfitting the second largest building in the world with a staff of Robot Depot robots. When Blitzer said that all of the bots assembled on the same floor for no reason just prior to the explosion, my stomach sank along with the building.

"Mike, here's a critical question," Phil Townsend said. "Is there a way to gather all of the bots in the same place at the same time, just like Blitzer said?"

"Sure. Every floor in the building has a chip in the wall that communicates with the bots. All you need to do is send out a signal to all of the machines and they'll come running like a bunch of border collies. But why would anybody do that other than to gather the bots for maintenance? Rick Bellamy will want the answer, and so do I."

"How the hell can a bunch of fucking bots cause an explosion that can take down a gigantic skyscraper?" Jenny wondered.

"Just like the floor cleaning bots caught on fire and destroyed five houses, a robot can be tampered with to become a bomb. Assume that all 360 of the Jameston Building bots were rigged to explode, and put them all in a room with flammable materials. The result is one gigantic explosion. It wasn't just a fire, it was a huge blast according to a ton of eyewitnesses."

"So in the last 24 hours we've gone from Robot Depot, the Bot People, to Robot Depot, the Bomb People," Jenny said. "Do you think that pervert Beekman has anything to do with this?"

"I doubt it," I said. "He doesn't want to kill us. He wants to drain money from us."

"It's a good thing you're friends with this FBI guy Bellamy," Phil said.

"It's always a good thing to have friends, but you'll notice something about Bellamy," I said. "He's an old-fashioned guy with complete integrity, and he follows clues wherever they take him. If the clues lead to his mother he'd bust her, after giving her flowers and a kiss."

The intercom buzzed. "A Mr. Bellamy and some other gentlemen are here to see you, Mike. He said you were expecting him," said Dianne the receptionist, a real human being. It sucks not to use robot receptionists because we're trying to push the sales of the machines for that purpose, and we look pretty dumb when we don't use them ourselves. But Blanche is right, as usual. Under our new circumstances, we need receptionists who can solve problems, not just relay messages.

Rick Bellamy walked in with six other guys in dark suits.

"Holy shit, why didn't you bring a fucking battalion while you're at it?" Jenny asked politely.

"I just want to be cautious in case you guys try to make a break for the door," Rick said. He may be a by-the-rules FBI agent, but he's got a sense of humor.

"Do you mind if my guys look around, Mike?"

"Mr. Bellamy," Phil said. "Do you have a subpoena or a search warrant?"

"That's okay, Phil. They don't need any of that stuff. I want to get to the bottom of this as much as they do." I grabbed the PA microphone.

"Attention everybody, it's Mike Bateman. Some gentlemen from the FBI will be wandering around asking questions. Give them your complete cooperation, but whatever you do, don't try to fix them up with a female droid."

They all cracked up. The fact that any of us can laugh after the events of the past 24 hours amazes me.

"Phil, I know that you're the attorney for Mike and Robot Depot, so please jump in if you have a problem with any of my questions. And please call me Rick."

"Rick, my marching orders from my client are to allow any questions at all. If I interrupt it will be to add to the conversation or to clarify something."

"Mike," Rick said, "when we spoke earlier I said that it seems obvious that somebody's out to fuck you, and after the Jameston Building disaster this morning, I'm sure of it. So here's my question, and I think it's your question too. Who is doing this? A competitor? Somebody from your past you may have slighted? A religious nut who thinks robots are Satan's doing? A terrorist? Think, Mike. Who hates you or Robot Depot?"

⊷ ⊶

"Mike, it's Jack Winston from quality control for you on line three," Dianne said. "He's at our store in Los Angeles today." Winston does quarterly visits to all of our stores.

Bellamy raised his hand to get my attention. "Tell him you'll call him right back, Mike."

"Tell Jack I'll get back to him shortly, Dianne."

"Tell me about your quality control system, Mike, and also tell me about Jack Winston."

"As you can imagine, Rick, quality control is a key part of our operation. We don't ever want word to get out that we sold a defective bot."

"Or an exploding one?" Rick said.

"Well, obviously. The way it works is that Jack Winston has a team of seven people who visually and electronically inspect every product before it leaves this plant. They literally take the thing apart to inspect it before giving the thumbs up. I know that you have your doubts about Winston, but he suspects an inside job too, and an inside job would mean one of *his* people. Rick, I can't imagine how it's not an onsite operation. We not only sell our own stuff through our retail outlets; we wholesale to other retailers. In the case of those cleaning bots catching fire, it's inconceivable that some bad guy could have placed saboteurs at all of the outlets where Robot Depot products are sold. It just doesn't make sense. Angus is equally emphatic that it's an inside job."

"Angus?" Bellamy said.

"You'll meet him shortly, Rick. Angus is a breakthrough in robotics and artificial intelligence. It, or he, is actually sentient."

"Sentient? Isn't that the difference between androids and human beings? You mean this Angus machine is aware of its own existence?"

"You've been doing your homework, Rick. Yes, Angus will change the way we think about ourselves. Hey, let me return Jack Winston's call. I'll put him on speaker."

"Does the name George Livingston ring a bell with you, Mike?" Jack Winston said.

"Isn't he on your team, Jack?"

"He is, or was. For the three years he's been with us he's never missed a day of work. He doesn't even take vacation days. Well, this morning I got a call that he didn't show up for work. I had my assistant call him to see if everything was okay. His phone was disconnected. His address is 25 Maple Street in Bay Shore. I suggest that one of those FBI guys you're talking to check out his house. Also, if the FBI is questioning people, make sure to ask about Livingston. Something is not adding up, Mike."

"I've got a guy on a case in Brightwaters which is next to Bay Shore," Bellamy said. "He can shoot over to Livingston's house in minutes."

Bellamy then called a judge to ask for a search warrant for Livingston's house. Within five minutes Bellamy received the warrant by encrypted email. Rick then looked at me.

"You're not the only fan of technology, Mike. What you just saw happen used to take a day or more."

Rick then phoned his guys on the floor below to tell them to ask about George Livingston. He also called his assistant at 26 Federal Plaza to run a background check on Livingston.

"What kind of background checks do you run on prospective employees, Mike?"

"Nothing as serious as an FBI background investigation, but we use a company that does a good job of tracking down people's histories. We don't want to hire thieves, drunks, druggies, or sexual prowlers."

A few minutes later Rick got a call from the agent with the search warrant in Bay Shore. He put his phone on speaker.

"All the furniture appears to be here, Rick," the agent said, "but the place is a wreck. It looks like somebody packed fast and moved out faster. I'm filling boxes with literature I found lying about. Wait, this looks like a trap door leading somewhere."

The last thing we heard was a loud blast.

CHAPTER TWENTY-FOUR

The Norwegian Cruise Line ship *Song of the Waves*, cast off its lines from the dock on the West Side of Manhattan. As the ship glided down the Hudson River, the sound system played Frank Sinatra singing *New York, New York*. The ship's destination was Bermuda.

Walter Brighton, the ship's captain, had recently been hired by Norwegian. Trained as an engineer, Brighton prided himself by being up to date on the latest technology. Six months before this cruise, he attended a robotics trade show in Miami sponsored by Robot Depot. He felt like a kid on Christmas morning. With facts, figures, graphs and charts, he convinced the suits at Norwegian headquarters that robotics was the way of the future and it may as well start now. He showed the Norwegian executives how he could save over $2 million a year by using robots on one ship alone. They picked the *Song of the Waves* as a test ship to try out Brighton's robot ideas. He purchased 14 floor cleaning robots, one for each deck. The bots were programmed to say hello anytime a passenger came within two feet. He also invested in two outside deck cleaning bots.

He was skeptical of using metallic machines in a salt water environment but the sales people from Robot Depot assured him that the stainless steel machines could take what the splashing waves had to offer. One of his favorite robots was a humanoid greeter bot that welcomed people to the buffet dining hall. Besides saying hello in three different languages, the bot dispensed antiseptic hand wipes to fight germs, always a concern on a cruise ship. Another of his favorite robots was located on the bridge. The bot was the size of a short person, standing at four feet tall. It reminded him of R2-D2, the famous *Star Wars* robot. By looking down at its top, one could see the ship's position, the depth, speed and arrival time to the next port. Of course all of these instruments were already on the bridge, but with the navigational bot everything was in one tidy bundle. He named the machine Magellan. In all, the *Song of the Waves* carried 20 robots.

The ship's entertainment director suggested that passengers call all of the floor cleaning robots Robbie. Captain Brighton thought this idea was dumb, but he couldn't come up with a better name himself, so Robbie was it. Magellan was the navigation bot, Betty Bot, the dining room greeter, Splashy, each of the exterior cleaning bots, and Sparky, the engine room bot.

Frank and Martha Johnston walked down the passageway to head for breakfast. With them were their twin five-year-old daughters, Megan and Alice. They came upon one of the floor cleaning bots as they rounded the passageway on the way to the elevator. "Hello Robbie," little Alice said.

The robot didn't answer as they expected, so both girls said, "Hello, Robbie."

"Fuck off, assholes," Robbie said.

Megan screamed and hugged Alice. Martha gently pushed them along the corridor. Frank gave the bot a kick as he passed it.

Betty Bot, the dining room welcoming robot, stood at her duty station, passing out disinfectant wipes and saying "good morning" to the passengers as they walked by. Betty's appearance was definitely robotic, but it was designed to present a friendly image. She was equipped with rose colored cheeks the size of baseballs, eyes the size of small saucers, which also sported blinking eyelashes. She wore a perma-smile, even when her banana sized lips moved as she spoke.

"Good morning," Betty Bot said, "please take a wipe and fight germs before they fight you."

"Goddamit, what the hell is this?" yelled the first woman who entered the dining hall. Her shout was repeated by everyone who followed her.

"This feels like battery acid," said an elderly man, a retired car mechanic.

One of the ship's mates, a human being, saw the commotion and approached Betty Bot. "Secure," he shouted, *secure* being the programmed command to any bot to shut down its activities and await further instructions. Betty Bot did not secure, but waved a disinfectant wipe in front of the mate. "Good morning. Please take a wipe and fight germs before they fight you."

He grabbed the wipe, then yelled "Shit, what is this stuff," as he dropped the wipe to the floor and waved his hands to dry them and relieve the pain. Betty Bot said nothing, but just reached out to him with another wipe.

"Secure," the mate shouted again. Betty kept greeting other passengers and waving wipes at them. The mate turned around toward the entrance and yelled to the crowd to avoid the robot, and not to take a wipe. A woman in gym clothes, who did not speak English, grabbed a wipe and rubbed it on her face. She screamed and cursed in her native tongue.

"Bridge, this is Eduardo Gomez in front of the main dining hall. The dining room robot is out of control and is passing out disinfectant wipes soaked in some sort of burning substance. The bot does not respond to the 'secure' command."

Two other crewmembers reported to Gomez, who positioned them 10 feet in front of Betty Bot, warning people away. Gomez looked down at his hands, which were covered by a bright red rash. The pain was excruciating.

⚒ ⚒

The first officer on the bridge glanced down at the top of Magellan, the navigation bot, to check on the depth. "Holy shit, Captain, we're about to go aground."

"All engines stop," Captain Brighton barked to the engine room. "All engines back full."

The ship had been steaming at 20 knots. Normally, if the captain wanted to stop the vessel he would do so in gradual stages to ensure safety and passenger comfort. The sudden stopping and reversing of all engines caused the ship to lurch violently, hurling passengers to the deck, and depositing hundreds of breakfast trays in various directions, splashing hot coffee and food on anyone in the way.

The captain looked at the top screen on Magellan, and then walked over to the regular sonar repeater.

"That blasted robot indicates a depth of seven feet under us, but sonar shows 400 feet. Get that goddam thing off the bridge."

"Captain, we have another problem," said the first officer. "Eduardo Gomez, the mate assigned to the dining room this morning, reports that the greeter robot, I think it's called Betty Bot, is acting erratically. Well, it's more than erratic; it's dangerous. The bot has been handing out disinfectant wipes soaked in a burning caustic substance. There's a line of people outside sick bay complaining of burns."

"Did he secure the robot?" Captain Brighton asked.

"The robot wouldn't respond to the *secure* command, sir," the first officer said. "Gomez thought fast and got the deck crew to wrap the thing up in chains."

"Beautiful, just beautiful," Brighton said. "Every passenger showing up for breakfast will be greeted by a fucking robot in chains. At least the damn thing can't talk anymore."

"Well, that's not quite so, Captain," said the first officer. "They can't figure out a way to turn the thing off, so it's still saying hello to people, although it can't give them wipes."

"Where did we buy these goddam robots," Captain Brighton asked of nobody in particular. He knew the answer, because the whole robot thing was his idea. I'll be lucky to command a canoe after this fiasco, he thought.

"Get me the number of the Robot Depot headquarters in New York," he said to one of the mates.

⊶⊷

"Mike, I can't believe this, but a cruise ship captain is calling from the middle of the friggin ocean," Dianne the receptionist said. "He sounds really pissed about something."

"By any chance is the ship the *Song of the Waves*?" I asked.

"Yes it is. Didn't we sell them a robot crew a couple of months ago?"

"We sure did, Dianne, we sure did," I said, a familiar knot forming in my stomach.

"This is Mike Bateman, how may I help you?"

I never knew an Englishman who could hurl four-letter words like this guy. He was so angry he could hardly speak. When he calmed down to a shout, he told me about the floor cleaning bots hurling foul language at children, a greeter bot handing our disinfectant wipes soaked in a caustic substance, and a navigation bot that erroneously announced they were about to go aground.

"The bottom line, Mr. Bateman, is this: Not only do your robots not work properly but they malfunction in outrageous and dangerous ways, bad enough to ruin a cruise for our passengers, who are

108

going to want answers from Norwegian Cruise Line. Your robots are supposed to help our parent company to turn a better profit. Instead, these pieces of shit are going to cost us a fortune in legal settlements."

"Captain, I believe you said that you expect to arrive in Hamilton, Bermuda, tomorrow. I will have a team of our engineers meet you. Please don't tamper with any of the robots until we inspect them."

"Tamper with them? My crew is afraid to go anywhere near the goddam things."

"All I can say, Captain, is that you shouldn't worry about the money you spent."

Captain Brighton felt relieved that the mayhem was coming to an end.

They would dock in Bermuda the next morning and the Robot Depot people would be there to handle the situation. At least we're done with robot surprises for now, he thought.

"What in holy hell was that?" Brighton bellowed to his first officer.

"It sounded like an explosion in the engine room, Captain."

Oh shit, thought Brighton. Sparky, the engine room bot.

"Captain this is Third Officer Margolis," yelled the voice over the intercom. "There's been an explosion in the engine room. The sprinkler system extinguished the fire, but we have no engine power."

"I've noticed, Mr. Margolis," said Brighton through gritted teeth, as the *Song of the Waves* drifted without power, taking sickening rolls from the waves.

⊷⊰⊹⊱⊶

"Sorry, Mike," Dianne said. "So how is your day going so far?"

"I'll let you know after I meet with our lawyers to review all of this shit."

CHAPTER TWENTY-FIVE

It was a miserable day. Heat, high humidity, and thundershowers, which didn't bring a break in the weather but only added to the sticky dampness. Nothing seemed to be going right. Even my dependable robocar, Carly, was not herself. On the way to the office I directed Carly to stop by Blanche's office to give her a ride. It was Blanche's first ride in Carly, and she loved it—for a few blocks. The car started bucking, snapping our heads back and forth. We noticed a weird odor.

"Hey, Carly, is everything okay?"

"I think I'm having transmission problems, Mike. Actually, I'm sure of it. After I drop you off, I recommend that you get alternate transportation to go home. I'll arrange for a truck to take me to the repair shop."

Carly dropped us off under the porte-cochere at the main entrance. The port-cochere was Jenny's idea when we constructed the building. At least my foul mood wouldn't be accompanied by rain- soaked clothing. Jenny was waiting for us in my office. She drove her own car because she had a dentist appointment that afternoon and didn't want to take Carly. She didn't know that Carly was sick.

Jenny, Blanche, and I went to the conference room to wait for Phil Townsend. Phil said he wanted to introduce us to a guy who would soon become a big part of our lives—a civil defense attorney named Bob Gentile. It was still pouring outside, but the conference room balanced the outside nastiness with inside comfort. The conference table was 18 feet long, making it possible to conduct large meetings. In front of each seat was a small microphone recessed into the wood. The tan leather furniture, which Jenny selected, gave off a feeling of coziness. It was good that the room was so comfortable, because the subject of the meeting would be anything but.

Phil Townsend walked in with Bob Gentile. Phil, as in-house counsel, is not a courtroom lawyer. Like most companies, we hire outside attorneys to handle litigation matters.

Bob Gentile, 42 years old, is about 5'10" with dark brown hair. He's a bit overweight but you can't notice because he wears an expertly tailored $2,000 suit. Bob has a reputation as a tough litigator, and he sometimes took it as a personal affront when his client was wrongfully accused of something. He stood next to a grease board so he could jot notes of his major points.

"I've known you folks, especially Mike, for a long time," Bob Gentile said. "I've had clients that I wished I could dump, but that's not you. Robot Depot, the company that Mike Bateman built is, in my opinion, one of the finest corporations in the country, and also one of the most important. Robotics and artificial intelligence are our future, and thanks to Robot Depot, part of our present. I'm not the one to announce troubling news—you already know the crap that's going on. I met with FBI agent Bellamy, and I think he's right. Somebody's out to hurt you, but none of us knows why. Phil asked me to meet with you folks and explain what we're up against. Please keep in mind, that although I personally like you guys, my job here is not to put on a smiley face and make you feel good. My job is to let you know what we're facing, and it isn't pretty. Everybody seems to think that Robot Depot is being sabotaged, and I think that's accurate. In a way it's almost obvious. Let's start with the Beekman matter, the husband who's suing you because his robotic wife malfunctioned. As we all agree, the guy is a fucking lunatic, but he's represented by Wally Yaeger, a pit bull of a tort lawyer. I don't want to spend a lot of time talking about this asshole, but I'm telling you that I may recommend that we settle and get rid of him. His case is built on negligent infliction of emotional distress, that's negligent, not intentional. But it *is* a valid legal cause of action, and in the hands of a skilled huckster, like Yaeger, a jury could find against us. Last we heard, the plaintiff is seeing a psychiatrist regularly. I know all about this particular psychiatrist, a household pet of Yaeger's. The sign in front of his office should read 'whore for hire.' I think we should maneuver a quiet settlement, with a strong non-publicity agreement and a clause saying that we're not admitting a wrong. Okay, enough with Beekman. Now on to more serious stuff."

"Bob," Jenny said, "Do you think that Beekman is trying to sabotage us?"

"No, frankly, I think he's a neurotic fool who's looking to cash in against a big company. Yaeger, his lawyer, loves publicity, but something tells me that he may back down, given that this case has become the darling of late night comedians."

"The bigger problem is the exploding robots, and ones that malfunction in weird ways like on that cruise ship. I'm less concerned about a pervert having sex with a robot than I am about that one terrible day a few weeks ago. Five houses were set on fire which resulted in 12 deaths. Then the Jameston Building in Chicago went down just like the World Trade Center on 9/11. We've already been served with lawsuits from 20 plaintiffs, and the number will grow every day. They have an evidence problem, but I think it can be overcome. Because all of the allegedly exploding robots were almost destroyed, the evidence against us at this point is purely circumstantial. But the facts in the Jameston Building case are scary. All 360 of the building's robots gathered on an unoccupied floor that contained flammable substances. The plaintiffs will claim that we knew or should have known that somebody could cause the robots to congregate in one place and explode them. What worries me about all of these cases is that some publicity-hungry prosecutors may bring indictments for criminally negligent homicide in addition to civil lawsuits based on negligence. I said at the beginning of this talk that my job is to shoot straight with you guys, and that's exactly what I'm doing. Mike, you could be facing jail."

"But what if we can prove that it was sabotage?" I asked. "Jack Winston, our quality control guy, is convinced that these were inside jobs, and I think that Rick Bellamy of the FBI agrees with him. Hell, one of the key people from quality control, George Livingston, has disappeared from the face of the earth. As the FBI guy who searched his house said, 'It looks like somebody packed fast and moved out faster.' His statement was recorded."

"And what happened after he said that, Mike?"

"He was blown up by a booby-trapped bomb," I said. "You don't have to be a crime drama fan to see that all signs point to Livingston."

"Yes, the signs do point to Livingston," Gentile said, "but we have no proof, just speculation, logical speculation, but speculation nonetheless. And I can't take a deposition from a guy I can't find."

"Bob, what do you think the government makes out of all of this?" Blanche asked. "I'm not talking about small-time prosecutors who want headlines, but the federal government."

"Great question, Blanche. In my conversations with them they've been open with me, especially Bellamy. I'm convinced that they're thinking the same as us— sabotage. They're looking at the incidents as possible terrorist activity, and I think they're right. This whole mess is starting to stink of terror. But that doesn't get us off the hook. We still face potentially thousands of private plaintiffs as well as local DAs who want to blame it on a big bad corporation. Who the hell would they sue, besides us, ISIS? Don't forget what I told you about the law of negligence. Corporations act through people, and sometimes those people are bad guys while working for the corporation. It's called the law of agency. Unless I can convince a jury that the bad guy's actions were so bad that they amounted to a 'frolic of his own' as the law says, we could be held liable. And keep in mind that plaintiffs' lawyers don't give a rat's ass about this company, nor do politicians. I can picture any number of senators standing in front of the Robot Depot headquarters, saying 'all of these deaths were caused by one greedy giant,' while pointing to this building."

"Bob, you think that the FBI is on our side, so to speak," Jenny said. "Why don't we let them take the lead?"

"The FBI's job, as well-intentioned as it may be, is not to defend Robot Depot. Their job is to find the real bad guys, especially if they suspect terror, which they do."

"I want to go non-stop public with this sabotage story," Blanche said. "I want to get the public on our side. We've got to get in front of this parade."

"No way in hell, Blanche," Gentile said. "We don't want to tip our hands to the real perpetrators that we suspect sabotage."

"Are you fucking kidding me?" Blanche yelled at the top of her voice. "Don't you think that the scumbags know we suspect sabotage? When a reporter asks Mike about the exploding bots what's he supposed to say? 'On the advice of counsel, I think I'll just stand here with my head up my ass?' Bob, we've got to get in front of this story, otherwise it will eat us alive."

Gentile was speechless. He looked chastened. Blanche sometimes shows wisdom way beyond her role as a public relations manager. She also has *chutzpa* to spare.

"So what about that, Bob?" I said. "I think Blanche makes a damn good point—the bad guys know that we suspect sabotage, so why play coy and let the press rule us? If I just stand there like an idiot and spout the bullshit about advice of counsel, the public trust in us will disappear, and the public trust means everything, not something, *everything*. As we go through this landmine of litigation we need to keep a big thing in mind: We've got to keep selling our products and generating income, otherwise it's lights out."

"Okay, okay," Bob said. "I'll admit that sometimes my lawyer thinking pushes aside my business thinking. Blanche, God bless her loud mouth, makes a tremendous point. Public relations is one of the battles in this war, and it's a battle we have to win. Mike, with the help of Blanche, I want you to come up with a memorized narrative for this mess. I just don't want you to ever say to a reporter, 'yeah, maybe we should have been more diligent with our quality control.' The narrative must say that Robot Depot has done everything it could to ensure the safety of our products, and that's the goddam truth so why not say it. Hey, Blanche, if you ever get tired of public relations, give me a call. I can make a hell of a litigator out of you, and I'll even give you a scholarship to law school."

Blanche was gracious, even though she just kicked this guy's ass.

"Thanks for the compliment, Bob. I did two years at NYU law school, so I know a little bit about the law."

"Why didn't you finish?" Bob asked.

"Too much bullshit. I'm sorry I bit your head off. I think all of us are on edge with this mess."

"You're not kidding, Blanche," Jenny said. "Even our car is sick."

CHAPTER TWENTY-SIX

The next day, Rick Bellamy surprised me by stopping by the office.

"You look like hell, my friend," Bellamy said. "Do you find something bothersome about the whole country bashing you on the head?"

I told him about the meeting with Bob Gentile the day before.

"We think that the FBI is totally focused on sabotage, Rick. I know *we* are, and I've decided to stop hiding it and go public with our suspicions. Care to comment?"

"Mike, you know I can't comment on that. I'd be giving you legal advice which I'm forbidden to do. But you also know about things that are obvious, so let's just leave it at that. I have a suggestion, and if you tell anyone I said this I'll deny it."

"So what's the suggestion, my secretive G-man friend?"

"Bennie Weinberg," Rick said.

"Who, pray tell, is he?"

"Bennie is a psychiatrist, recently retired from the New York City Police Department, where he was also a detective. Prosecutors worship the guy because he has an uncanny knack for spotting lies on the witness stand. His nickname is 'Bennie-the-Bullshit Detector.' Ben wrote a widely read book called *How to Spot Lies.* He is one smart guy, a graduate of Harvard Medical School no less. Mike, I think you'll agree that there's a lot of bullshit in your current circumstances. I suggest you contact this guy."

On Rick Bellamy's suggestion I called Dr. Benjamin Weinberg. Rick's right. There is a hell of a lot of lying going on, the most obvious being that guy Livingston from quality control who disappeared suddenly.

"Mike, a Dr. Benjamin Weinberg is here to see you. He's a little early."

"Send him in, Dianne." A little early. I like that.

A man dressed in an expensive suit walked in, smiled, and extended his hand. He asked me to call him "Bennie." He's about 5'10" a bit overweight with a balding head, which he did not try to cover with a comb-over.

"My wife, Maggie, thinks you're the most wonderful man in the world, Mike. She works out of our apartment as a writer, and she hates to have cleaning people buzzing about. But she loves her little family of time-saving robots from Robot Depot."

"Glad to be of service, Bennie," I said. It was easy to like this guy, I thought. He had a way about him that puts you at ease.

"Rick Bellamy is quite fond of you, Mike. I understand that the two of you grew up together. Rick tells me that you need some assistance in separating truth tellers from liars, is that right?"

"That's more than right, Bennie. We find ourselves surrounded by liars, people who are out to fuck us, as Rick puts it. He says that your nickname is 'Bennie-the-Bullshit-Detector.' And that sounds like the kind of guy I need right now."

"Mike, your company is exploding in front of our eyes. Rick Bellamy discussed a few things with me, but most of what I know about Robot Depot's problems comes from the newspapers and TV news in the last couple of weeks. You've gone from a cuddly consumer-friendly business to a mean capitalist monster overnight. You don't have to be a bullshit detector to know that something terrible is happening. Rick Bellamy's right. Somebody's out to fuck you. First we have to figure out why, then we need to figure out who. Then we need to fuck *them* before they do any more harm."

"I love that you're not just a shrink but a retired cop. You have the instincts that I don't. I wish I could help point you in the right direction, but for the life of me I have no idea who is doing this shit."

"That's why Rick wanted you to talk to me, Mike. I think I know *why* and I have a few ideas about *who*."

"You think you know who is behind this?" I said.

"I'm just speculating at this point, Mike, but if I'm correct, you haven't seen anything yet."

CHAPTER TWENTY-SEVEN

Mustaffa Ali and his friend, Muhammed Shumar, sat having tea in Ali's apartment in Queens. Ali goes by his "infidel" name Jim Flager, and Shumar is known as Walter Buono. On command from the management at ISIS, terrorists all over the world are hiding their identities so they can do their work in the shadows. Intelligence agencies all over the world refer to this new procedure as *The Shadows of Terror.*

"Are we ready to go, Walter?"

"We're ready right now, Jim, and by next Friday we blast off. The long range forecast is for perfect weather. That can change, of course, but we aren't stuck with one date."

"How many drones do we have?" asked Jim Flager

"Two hundred, Jim, a nice even number," Buono said.

"Have they all been modified?"

"Every last one of them. To be cautious, I've picked 10 different launch areas. That means only 20 drones will launch from each area. The drones we're using are the most silent on the market. Robot Depot does a great job with quality control."

They both laughed after Buono said that.

      —⇢⇤—

The Yankees versus the Mets is one of the most popular and well-attended games for New York baseball fans. This year's "subway series" will consist of three games played over three days from July 14 to July 16. The first game will be held at 7:10 p.m. at Yankee Stadium. Hugo Garcia, a pitching phenomenon the Yanks hired a week before, will take the mound for the Yankees. The crowd on the night of the first game would be a bit over 50,000, just shy of record attendance. The new Yankee Stadium was completed in April of 2009. The *House that Ruth Built* was replaced by the *House That George Built,* named after former Yankees owner, the late George Steinbrenner. Some call the new stadium the *House that Jeter Built,* after the Yankees great short stop and team captain, Derek Jeter.

      —⇢⇤—

"Hi Mike, it's Bennie Weinberg. I have three tickets to the Yankees-Mets first game of their series tomorrow night. Maggie's feeling under the weather and can't make it, and her sister doesn't want to go. How about I treat you and Jenny. With the amount of money you're paying me I can afford it."

Both Jen and I are big baseball fans, especially the Mets, so saying yes to Bennie was easy. We had a scheduled meeting with Bennie on Friday, so the three of us would leave from here, with Carly driving us to Yankee Stadium. Carly had her transmission repaired and was driving perfectly.

Friday, July 14 was a mild evening at about 78 degrees with low humidity, perfect weather to watch a baseball game.

Hugo Garcia, the new Yankees pitcher from Ecuador, stood on the mound warming up.

Bennie just returned to his seat with six hot dogs after visiting the food concession.

"As a doctor, I have to warn you not to eat these because I haven't the foggiest idea what's in them. But I simply can't imagine a ball game without hot dogs."

"What's that sound," Jenny said. "It's a low humming sound that's getting louder."

"I hear it," Bennie said. "It sounds like a bunch of model airplanes."

I looked up and saw a massive flight of drones passing over the edge of the stadium.

"Holy shit," I yelled, suddenly realizing what was about to happen. "Everybody under the seats" I screamed, "NOW, *RIGHT FUCKING NOW.* Cover your heads."

I had just positioned my chest over Jennie's head when the explosions began. I saw plenty of combat in the Marines, but I never heard so many explosions at one time. What we heard at Yankee Stadium was louder than anything I'd ever experienced. A wind storm of wood and pieces of metal swept through our seating area. We could hear debris strike the seats over our heads. I heard and felt a large crash just above me, and I didn't have to look. I knew it was a human body. The explosions continued for another five minutes. The sounds of the blasts were gradually replaced by the horrible sound of people screaming, including children, especially children. The three of us climbed out from under our seats and stood. I looked at the body of a teenage boy who had landed on my seat. He stared through dead eyes. Thank God we were all okay. Jennie reached up with a hanky to wipe blood off my forehead.

"I suggest that we stay exactly where we are and keep out of the way of the rescue teams," I said.

We stood with handkerchiefs over our faces to fend off the wind-carried dust and debris.

"Do you think those drones were ours, honey?"

"Yes, they were ours. Our drones have a distinctive sound to them."

The scene of devastation in front of us was sickening. Hundreds of broken bodies lay across the baseball field. Many of the bodies were in uniform. What was once the press box looked like it took a direct hit. It tilted sharply toward one side like an old car with a flat tire, poised to topple to the ground below. I could see players from both teams fanned out across the field helping the wounded. Hugo Garcia, the Yankees' newly acquired pitching ace, would never throw a pitch in a major league game. He lay dead on the mound.

"I'm an internist besides being a shrink," Bennie said as he dusted off his shirt. "I'm going down there to that first aid tent to help."

"We're right with you, Bennie," I said.

I spoke for Jen because I knew I didn't have to ask her if she wanted to help. Jenny's not one to wilt in front of danger, as I recalled her saving my life in Afghanistan. We followed Bennie to the first aid tent.

"I'm Doctor Ben Weinberg, and these are my friends. Where do you need us?"

What began as a night of fun turned into the ugliest evening of our lives. For hours the screaming never stopped. The cries of anguish came not only from wounded men, women, and children. The worst screams came from people whose kids were killed.

Seeing a dead body is a gruesome sight. But for some reason seeing body parts strewn about is even worse. I knew, as did everybody, that a few minutes ago, those arms, legs, and heads belonged to living human beings.

A sound truck pulled to the center of the field. The microphone was manned by somebody from the Red Cross, as best I could tell. Whoever it was had obvious experience and training for scenes of devastation like this. The person in charge of the first aid station asked Jen and me to help lead dazed but ambulatory people to the tent. One medivac helicopter after another landed to pick up the wounded to take them to area hospitals. As gratifying as it was to see the efficiency of the first responders, the rotor wash from the helicopters created a constant wind storm of debris.

By 1 a.m. all of the wounded had been evacuated, and the grim task of the body handlers continued. The three of us changed from our blood-stained clothes into clean garments provided by the Red Cross. We walked to the parking lot, and there was Carly, having escaped damage.

"I was a combat physician with the 82nd Airborne in the First Gulf War," Bennie said as we walked to the car. "I saw a lot of nasty shit, but nothing like I saw tonight. Mike, Jen, we've got to find the fuckers who are turning Robot Depot into a weapons factory."

"How, who?" Jen said.

"We need to sleep, obviously, but tomorrow I want to hunker down with you guys. I have some ideas about who may be creating this shit storm."

We dropped Bennie at his apartment on East 79th Street, and then told Carly to take us to our brownstone on East 86th. We planned to pick up Bennie and head out to Robot Depot headquarters in Hauppauge the following morning.

The three of us, all combat veterans, would later agree that the scene at Yankee Stadium was the worst horror any of us had ever experienced. Bennie couldn't stop talking about a little girl, maybe 10 years old, who died in his lap from a loss of blood, her arm having been ripped off. He also couldn't stop crying.

CHAPTER TWENTY-EIGHT

"Mike, it's Blanche. Dear God, I just found out that you and Jen were at the game last night. Are you two okay?"

"Our ears are still ringing from the explosions, but otherwise we're fine. We're in Carly heading to the office. We have a friend with us, Dr. Ben Weinberg, the guy I told you about. I know it's Saturday but can you meet with us later around two?"

"Of course, Mike. Hey, listen up. You may need to pull over for a TV interview on your cell phone. Shepard Smith from *Fox News* wants to interview you about the latest shit."

"You know something, Blanche, why don't you do the interview? I've seen you on TV before and I think you're great. We're all on the same page, so let the world hear from somebody other than Mike Bateman."

"You got it, Mike," Blanche said. "Your face is becoming associated with explosions. Somebody else should represent Robot Depot from time to time. I'm feeling composed, which I always am when I'm furious about something. I got to get ready for the interview. See you later."

"We'll be watching you on my iPad, Blanche," Jenny said.

"That's one tough PR lady you have there, Mike," Bennie said.

"You should hear her when she really gets worked up," I said.

"Mike, I'm surprised that you're letting Blanche handle this," Jenny said. "She's good, but I was sure you'd want to be heard yourself."

"I've been thinking about this a lot, and not just this morning. I'm becoming known as Mr. Death, CEO of the Robot Depot. You heard Blanche. She thought the same thing. Let the public know there's more to Robot Depot than me."

⇀⊹ ⊹↽

"Good morning, ladies and gentlemen, Shepard Smith reporting for *Fox News*. The toll of mayhem and the body count continues to mount. In just the past two weeks, we've seen five houses destroyed by exploding robotic floor cleaners, a giant skyscraper brought to the ground in Chicago, a cruise ship turned into a scene of floating chaos, and last night, the horrible drone attack on Yankee Stadium. Hundreds died and hundreds more are in hospitals, some not expected to live. What has law enforcement stumped, and the press as well, is that the common denominator in all of these robotic incidents is one company, Robot Depot, a business that happily calls itself, 'Your bot people.' We have with us, broadcasting from Robot Depot headquarters in Hauppauge, Long Island, a spokesperson for the company, Blanche Whiteacre."

Fox had sent a sound truck to Robot Depot. The cameraman and his assistance focused on Blanche, sitting in our main conference room.

"Blanche, can you help us out with any thoughts or opinions about what the heck is going on?" Smith said. "As you well know, and whether it's fair or not I don't have an opinion, but a lot of people are accusing Robot Depot of criminally negligent homicide or worse. Some are even saying that Robot Depot is complicit in terrorism. Please give us your thoughts."

"Shepard, it's inappropriate for me to say bullshit on live television, but that's the only word in the English language that covers the subject. Bullshit."

"Nobody has to tell Blanche how to kick ass," Jenny said, as we watched the interview on her iPad.

Smith, as well as the three of us in the car, laughed.

"Well thank you, Blanche, for waking up the guy on the delay button in our control booth. Rather than ask you to clean up your language, because I understand how upset you are, I'll ask you to express yourself as you feel natural, and our delay button guy will just get an ulcer."

Smith, a veteran reporter, had a visceral feeling for good TV. He figured he'd let Blanche hold forth, knowing that the network execs would never fire him for putting on a good show.

"The reason I used that word, Shepard, is because all facts point toward that conclusion" Blanche said. "Robot Depot is one of the most successful companies in manufacturing and retail, and there are assholes [*delay button*] out there who actually believe that we've turned into an evil monster. Law enforcement, including the FBI, are investigating these events, and a word that we keep hearing is 'sabotage,' That's right, some group is using Robot Depot to commit horrible crimes, and we have reason to believe that some of the activity may have been done by in-house traitors. That's right traitors, not just to Robot Depot, but traitors to the country itself. These shitheads [*delay button*] don't know who they're dealing with. When the scumbags [*delay button*] are finally arrested and brought to justice, I would love to see you interview them, Shepard."

"Wow," I said. "Blanche used the words 'Assholes, shitheads, scumbags.' Hey Jenny, have you been giving Blanche speech lessons?"

"I don't think she needs instructions," Jen said. "She's great, and I actually think Shepard Smith is getting a kick out of her vocabulary."

"So, Blanche, you're bringing us shocking news," Shepard Smith continued. "You're saying that the horrible crimes of the past few days are caused by saboteurs, not loyal Robot Depot employees."

"Yes, that's precisely what I'm saying. What we don't know is why and who, and that's why we're working closely with law enforcement."

"There you have it, ladies and gentleman, straight from Robot Depot's able spokesperson Blanche Whiteacre. Blanche, we hope to have you on again in the near future, but could you sprinkle your language with a few 'hecks,' 'darns,' and 'gee whizzes'?"

"No problem, Shepard, you can fuc... I mean friggin count on it." Blanche said.

CHAPTER TWENTY-NINE

As if I didn't have enough to worry about, this afternoon is the *Beekman* deposition at the office of his attorney, Wally Yaeger.

Jenny, Bob Gentile, Blanche, Bennie Weinberg, and I gathered in my office to prepare for the deposition. I wanted Bennie to assess the truthfulness of John Beekman, the robot lover.

"Bennie, please pass me the water pitcher," Bob Gentile said. "Thank you. You are now my assistant in case anybody asks. Yaeger may object to your presence at the deposition."

"You lawyers really are full of shit," Bennie said, laughing.

"Only when necessary, Ben."

We went over the evidence, although I thought the exercise was absurd. Yes, the lady robot came from us, and yes, it had a battery-charging problem. But what made me crazy was that we were involved in a lawsuit with a guy who was angry with us for screwing up his romance with a robot.

"I've been making inquiries and doing some research as Bob requested," Blanche said. "This guy Beekman is a three dollar bill. He's been married four times, not counting his current wedded state to a machine. He was arrested once for masturbating in front of a doll store. You can't make this shit up. When our people examined the robot, which he brought in for repairs, they found these pink panties on the bot. Maybe Bob wants to return them to Mr. Beekman at the deposition."

Laughing, Bob took the panties and put them in his briefcase.

"I just may do that, Blanche."

"Our only legal obligation is to repair his robot wife, or replace it if the repairs don't work," Gentile said. "I understand that we've fixed the robot's battery compartment, so in the interest of getting rid of this case, I'm going to offer him the fixed-up bot in exchange for a release."

"What's the demand?" Jenny asked.

"Ten million. If Yaeger pushes the issue I think we should offer him a brand new android to replace his 'wife.' He's been married enough times that I don't think he'll have a hard time adjusting to yet another spouse."

Beekman and his attorney, Wally Yaeger, were waiting for us when we entered the conference room where the deposition would be held. The room, about 40 by 50 feet, was stark modern, and obviously decorated without the aid of an interior designer. The furniture was cheap shit, the kind that you find in a lousy diner. It was garish green, threadbare in spots, and the walls looked as if they hadn't been painted in years. I guessed he wanted a 'man of the people' décor. I sat down next to Jenny on a chair equipped with a big rip on the seat. As Bob Gentile predicted, Yaeger objected to the presence of everyone except me and Bob. As we planned, we would settle for just Bennie and Jen to be there. Blanche would have to go. I felt bad for her because I could tell that she looked forward to a fun deposition.

After the legal preliminaries, including oath taking and signing documents, the deposition began, with Bob Gentile questioning Mr. Beekman.

"Mr. Beekman, did there come a time when you came into possession of a robot that you believe was manufactured and sold by my client Robot Depot?"

"I never knew she was a robot." Beekman said.

"What is her name?"

"Gloria."

"Did you give her that name or did she tell you?"

"She told me her name was Gloria."

Shit, I wished Blanche could be here to see this.

"Did you have intimate sexual contact with Gloria?"

Objection," Yaeger shouted. "Irrelevant and immaterial."

"Counselor," said Bob, trying to suppress a laugh, "I'm trying to establish the time when your client came to the belief that Gloria was a human being."

"Yes, I had sex with Gloria," said Beekman without waiting for his attorney to respond to Bob. He seemed to want to tell us about it.

"When you said that you had sex, sir, did that include full sexual intercourse including penetration?" Bob Gentile asked, trying desperately not to laugh.

"Of course. It was a wonderful experience."

Bob reached into his briefcase and withdrew the pink panties.

"This garment belongs to your client. We found these panties on the robot known as Gloria."

"Objection," shouted Yaeger. "The defense has shown no chain of custody for this garment."

"I'll be happy to provide you with written statements or a live deposition of the Robot Depot employees who found the panties on Gloria," Gentile said. "I have no further questions."

Bob Gentile got the only testimony that he really wanted, a statement about the impossible. There's simply no place to insert anything into the robot. Bob considered the case closed at this point, he would later tell me. Yaeger looked like he'd been hit by a truck. Now it was his turn to depose me. Yaeger focused his eyes on mine with a piss load of theatricality.

"Mr. Bateman, are you the CEO of Robot Depot?"

As coached by Bob, I answered without any emotion, even though I wanted to punch this asshole. So I answered, "yes."

"Do you care at all about the quality of the robots that you sell to the public?"

"Objection," Bob Gentile said, "you're asking the witness for an opinion."

"Counselor, are you suggesting that Mr. Bateman doesn't care about the products he sells?"

This guy Yaeger really is a dick, as Bob had warned me.

"I'm not suggesting anything, Mr. Yaeger, all I'm asking is that you conform your questions to the law."

"To the best of your knowledge, did there come a time when your company, Robot Depot, released into the stream of commerce a female-appearing android bearing the model number B3205?"

"If by 'stream of commerce,' you're asking me if we sold that robot, the answer is yes, but we did not sell it directly to your client."

"How many of these sexually attractive androids do you sell in a given year?"

"Objection," Gentile shouted. "If you find these machines sexually attractive, that's your business. Please do not pose such a ridiculous question to Mr. Bateman."

"Okay, without expressing any opinion of the robots, how many did you sell last year?"

"The answer is one—one female android," I said.

The deposition became as crazy as I expected. Unless Yaeger was able to come up with something surprising, I saw this case as over.

"What is the purpose of this android, Mr. Bateman? Is it not as a sex partner?"

Bob was about to object, but he just laughed and said to me, "Go ahead and answer."

"No, Mr. Yaeger, the purpose of the android is *not* to serve as a sex partner, but for use as a receptionist or greeter at a business. If you physically examine the robot you will see that your question doesn't make sense. You can no sooner have sex with a park bench than you can with the android." I violated Bob's warning against giving more of an answer than what was asked, but I couldn't resist.

"I have no further questions," Yaeger said.

As we were walking out of the room, Yaeger called Bob Gentile over to the side.

"My final demand is $1 million, but that's only if we can settle it today."

"And here's my offer," Bob Said. "We'll replace the android, but after we subtract for the cost of repairs that we already performed. If you don't accept my offer, I'll put the case on the trial calendar and we'll see what a jury thinks of your client's broken marriage to a robot. But before we even get that far I'm going to make a Motion for Summary Judgment based on the testimony we heard today. I'm going to ask the court to throw this case out."

"Good day, sir," Yaeger said.

"Well, Bennie," Bob Gentile said. "Were these two telling the truth?"

"Yaeger was lying through his teeth, but you expected that. For him the truth is how much money he can extract from a defendant. Beekman, on the other hand, is an interesting case. He's a garden variety psychopath. He actually believes that Robot Depot did him wrong with a faulty robot. He even believes he had sex with the damn thing. I loved Mike's comment about having sex with a park bench. Beekman wasn't lying in a way that could be seen as perjury. The nut really believes this shit."

"Mike, it's Bob Gentile for you on line three," said Dianne the next morning. "He sounds extremely happy about something."

"I just got off the phone with Yaeger," Bob said. "After he and his client got the shit kicked out of them yesterday, he decided to accept reality. He's dismissing the case on his own motion in exchange for the fixed-up robot. You now have one less thing to worry about, Mike."

One less thing, according to Bob Gentile, I thought. *One less thing.*

CHAPTER THIRTY

"Jen, wake up," I shouted. She didn't awaken so I shook her. When she opened her eyes, I didn't have to tell her what was wrong. Our house was on fire. I don't remember where, but I recalled seeing a video warning you to keep your bedroom door closed at night. After we watched that video, keeping the bedroom door closed became a habit with us. We could see the orange glow at the base of the door and could actually hear the flames roaring on the other side.

Our bedroom overlooked a sloping roof.

"That window," I yelled. I knew enough about fires to realize that when I opened the window, whatever flames were in the hallway would come at us from under the door like a blast furnace. We had to move fast. I grabbed my cellphone off the table next to the bed. Then I opened the window and helped Jen onto the roof. I followed her onto the roof and quickly closed the window behind me. The roof we stood on was one story high, with evergreen trees just below the roofline.

"Let's do it," I said. "Aim for the middle of that tree." We both jumped and neither of us was injured except for scrapes. I looked up and saw that the entire house was becoming engulfed in flames. We ran about a hundred feet into the yard and I called 911 on my cell phone. As I was pressing the buttons we could hear the sound of fire engines pulling up the block. Apparently an alert neighbor had already spotted the fire.

A fireman ran up to us with a couple of blankets, which we hardly needed on the warm July night. We knew the guy, a neighbor and member of the volunteer fire department.

"Are you guys okay?" he asked. "Any pain in your chests? Scratchy throat?"

I told him we had our bedroom door closed, so we didn't inhale any smoke.

"That's why you're alive," the fireman said. "I've seen enough dead bodies in rooms with the door left open."

Sam and Laura Braun, our next-door neighbors, invited us into their house. They loaned us some clothes to replace our fire department blankets. As we sipped coffee in their kitchen we heard a loud crashing sound. When we looked out the window we could see that our house was now a pile of flaming rubble, the roof having collapsed.

The four of us walked to the main pumper truck, where the fire chief stood, shouting orders. We knew him well from the neighborhood.

"Hi Mike, Hi Jenny," he said. "The police are sending their arson squad. Even though the fire isn't completely doused, it looks suspicious. It looks like accelerants were used in four areas of the first floor. In each of those areas are remnants of machines of some sort that look like floor cleaning robots. From the way I see it, I'm betting that the fire started in those four locations. I don't want to be dramatic with you folks, but it looks to me like somebody wanted you both dead."

CHAPTER THIRTY-ONE

O ur house burned down two days ago as a result of arson, not an accident. The arson squad confirmed the fire chief's suspicion that four areas were set up with accelerants, and in each area they found the charred remains of a floor cleaning robot, one of whom was "Dusty," a bot we thought of as an old friend.

Jen and I moved into the guest cottage on our property. Fortunately the flames didn't reach the cottage. We did some quick shopping to replace all of our clothes that went up in flames. For the first time in our lives, we've been tailed by bodyguards.

"Rick Bellamy, that FBI guy, is here to see you, Mike," Dianne said.

It was 10 a.m. and Jen and I were sitting in my office with Blanche, Bennie Weinberg, and Phil Townsend. It was more like a war council than a meeting. Because of the exploding robot incidents of the past few weeks, I had ordered increased security for our headquarters, our manufacturing plant, and all of our stores. One of our board members made a motion during an Internet meeting that the company pay for private security guards for Jen and me. The motion carried unanimously.

"Good morning, everybody," Bellamy said. "Robot Depot, you may be pleased to know, is now the most critical file in our office. Mike, when these incidents first started, I ventured the opinion that somebody is out to fuck you. That's no longer speculation, but the truth, the obvious truth. Now, the only question is exactly who."

"Rick, after our house burned to the ground I no longer doubt that somebody is looking to shut us down, and I don't just mean just the company, but Jenny and me. I still don't have a clue as to who would do this."

"That's what I'm here for. It's now officially an FBI matter, and that wasn't just my idea. The White House wants to know what the hell is going on. President Trump is quite fond of you, Mike. Apparently you got to know each other before he was elected. He sees Robot Depot as one of America's great companies, and I can't say I blame him. I'm sure he's going to Tweet about his feelings. You're on the cutting edge of the new economy. So today we're going to focus on possible suspects. I made up a list of ideas that I want to share with you people. Mike, please tell us what you think are the main areas of suspicion."

"Competitors," I said. "I know that we're brainstorming, but I think that's a long shot. We have about three serious competitors, and I've shared that info with you guys at the FBI. But we're really friendly with the competition. Yeah, we're giants compared to them, but they provide us with additional retail outlets, and they help spread the word that robots are good and useful things. I think they all expect a phone call with an offer to buy them out some day, and that may just happen. I already opened the subject with our anti-trust lawyers.

"A jilted lover, is suspect number two. Jenny's my only lover, and I'd rather blow myself up than sneak around. What about a jilted lover of a key employee? I simply cannot believe that somebody would cause such death and destruction just because a former boy or girlfriend works for us. It doesn't make sense.

"The next area of suspicion is a disgruntled employee. Again, I try to look at the logic. I'm sure that over the years somebody has parted company from us not under the best of terms. I've also shared those names with the FBI, and they haven't found anything. I'm going to let Rick Bellamy talk about our fourth area of suspicion. Rick?"

"I almost hate to say this because it sounds too big to fight," said Bellamy, "but it's where we're dragged by the facts and logic. The prime suspect is terrorism, specifically the Islamic State or ISIS. The depravity of the attack on Yankee Stadium leads us to that hypothesis."

"Why the hell would a terrorist group want to focus on a specific company?" Phil Townsend asked said.

"Bennie, I think you're the best one to answer Phil's question," Bellamy said.

"I have worked on enough cases involving ISIS or al Qaeda to know that we can't figure out the *why* until we've discovered the *what*," Bennie said. "In other words, what are they looking to accomplish? Then we'll figure out why, if that's important. From my study of Islamist extremism, and I've studied it a lot, I think that the jihadis see robots as somehow anti-religious, mimickers of God so to speak. They see it as another case of infidels indulging in idolatry. So what better way to avenge the idolatry than to make the robots destroy their creators."

"Jenny and I realized something," I said, "something pretty scary. The arson squad determined that four fires started downstairs in our house, and each of the four areas was occupied by a burnt-out robot. It's the same set of facts as in those five houses that burned down a few weeks ago. Here's the scary part. We brought all four of those bots into our house three years ago—*three* years ago. All of a sudden, a few days ago, the bots erupted into flames, a week after those other house fires. Anybody want to venture a guess as to how many of those kind of bots we've sold in the past three years? The answer is that we've sold 450,000 robotic floor cleaners all over the world. Remember that movie, *The War of the Worlds*? In that flick, gigantic machines that were buried for thousands of years are awakened by lightning bolts to reap destruction. Well, just working off the facts about our house, the time span isn't thousands of years, but at least three— *At least*. It could be longer. So what I'm telling you folks is that there could be a gigantic number of our bots waiting for a signal to blow up. We don't know how the explosions were triggered, but at least we have something to focus on. It makes me sick to say this, but based on what we know, there are thousands of ticking time bombs out there. We did some quick calculations, and found out that since the explosions in the five houses two weeks ago, followed up by the Jameston Building in Chicago, followed by the sabotaged cruise ship, followed by the drone attack at the Yankee Stadium, followed by our house burning down five days ago, and all of a sudden I think we have a national emergency. I agree with Rick Bellamy that it looks like terrorism. What the hell else could it be? The operation, so far, covers a wide territory and it was executed with a high level of sophistication. Need I mention the thousands of deaths and injuries, and billions of dollars in property damage? I think we know what we have to do. We need to launch the biggest product recall in the history of business. Rick, your thoughts?"

Bellamy stared at the floor for a few moments, uncharacteristic for him. He shook his head and looked at me.

"Mike, you and I have been friends for a long time, although I shouldn't say that in front of other people. But you're right. You need to send out a worldwide recall announcement, and then we'll try to see how those robots were turned into bombs. The negative press against your company will be relentless, but you have a big thing on your side. You didn't do anything wrong or duck any responsibility. I leave it to your talented PR lady here to put that message out to the consumer."

"I love working under pressure, Rick," Blanche said. "Pardon me while I go to the ladies room and barf."

"I've ordered increased security which started yesterday," I said. "I've also put in place enhanced quality control. Not one bot will ever leave our manufacturing facility without being pulled apart and inspected. We don't want to release any more time bombs on the world."

CHAPTER THIRTY-TWO

"Billy, we've got to repurpose Angus for the time being," I said to our chief scientist as I walked into his office.

"I expected you to say that, Mike. It's obvious to anybody that a lot of nasty shit is going on. What are your thoughts?"

"The FBI thinks it's terrorism and I agree with them. Because all of the events involve Robot Depot products, it's *our* problem not just a law enforcement issue. But we have a secret weapon, and his name is Angus. You've invented an amazing robot, Billy, and I think he can get a handle on this crap faster than we can. I've seen him diagnose some complicated medical cases, and I want to turn him loose on our problem."

"Mike, from what you've told me, especially after your house burned down, we have a problem with quality control, and the problem goes back years. It's possible that our products all over the world that are waiting to explode."

"You're the smartest guy I've ever met, Billy, next to Angus. That's why you're our chief scientist."

"Thanks for the compliment, Mike. Yes I am proud that I invented a machine that's smarter than me. So let's boil this stew down to its ingredients. First, we have to figure out how the timing devices or remote detonators work. Then we need to figure out a way to disable the mechanisms. I'm going to suggest that you hold off on the giant recall until we can find out what exactly we're dealing with from an engineering point of view. If you issue the recall, whoever the bad actors are can wait for them to come into our plants and then blow the goddam things up, killing a lot of our best people. If you were a terrorist out to kill Robot Depot, isn't that what you'd do? It only makes sense. Let's huddle with Angus now."

⟞⟝ ⟞⟝

"Hello, Angus," I said. I'm one of a few people in the world who thinks it's normal to talk to a robot.

"Good afternoon, Mike, good afternoon, Billy. I have been hearing and reading about the difficulties facing Robot Depot. I've concluded that the problem is one of terrorism."

"It doesn't surprise me that you're right up to speed with our thinking," I said. "Please give us your analysis of the situation, and we'll see where we go from here. Think of it like one of those medical cases you diagnosed. Our company is sick, and I want you to diagnose the problem and recommend a solution. But first let me give you two pieces of information. One, all of the violent events of the past few weeks are the result of one or more of our robots exploding or malfunctioning. Second, and this is the scary part. Based on the facts surrounding my house burning down, we know that we've sold at least three years' worth of products which may contain exploding mechanisms."

Angus slowly nodded his new humanoid head up and down, emitting a slight whirring sound.

"Here is where I see the situation at the present," Angus said. "First, I knew that there is some sort of explosive device inside many of our products. I did not know the second fact until now, that there are possibly thousands of our tampered-with products in use for at least three years. That certainly provides us with a sense of urgency. We need to consider a third factor. Until we know the exact nature of the explosive device and the timer or remote control switch, we can't inspect those machines for defects, for the obvious reason that the inspector may be killed if he digs too deeply into the mechanism. Not a reasonable option. I must devise a method for inspecting the machines without actually tampering with them, a challenging but not insurmountable problem. The time right now is 5 p.m., approaching what human beings call quitting time. I will address these issues overnight, which should be plenty of time for me to come up with some solutions because I don't require sleep. I recommend that you gentlemen go home and do that thing that humans do, have sex with your spouse or partner. My research tells me that human beings are most efficient when they are relaxed. So, as I believe you'd put it, go home and get laid. I have no idea why humans find rubbing naked bodies against one another to be relaxing, but it seems to work, from what I've read. I will see you in the morning at 9 a.m. or at any other time that Mike chooses."

"Angus, every time I talk to you I feel like I've just received an education," I said. "We'll see you in the morning at nine."

CHAPTER THIRTY-THREE

"Hey, Jen, it's quitting time. Let's leave."

"But it's only 5:30, Mike. Don't you have more to do? I know I do."

"I've got plenty to do, as usual, but I think it's a great idea to go back to the guest cottage and have sex."

"What? Why? I mean I'm not objecting, but the atmosphere today doesn't seem romantic."

"It's Angus' idea, Jen. He has analyzed human behavior and concluded that we work best when we're relaxed and not under stress. He says, not that he's got any experience, that sex calms us down and makes us more productive."

"Let me grab my purse. I think we need more robots like Angus."

⊱⊰

Jenny and I lay in bed, totally spent. Our guest cottage, located next to the creek, actually had a better view than our house, which would be under reconstruction for about six more months.

"Hey, do you realize it's still daylight on a stressful workday," Jenny said, "and we just behaved like it was the first night of our honeymoon. I think Angus is on to something. I feel wonderful, you?"

"I think it's because we just did something that we thought we shouldn't do. Screw in the daytime on an extremely busy workday. Makes it feel sort of naughty, no?"

"Naughty, yes," Jenny said. "How do you feel now?"

"I still feel naughty. Let's not waste good feelings."

"We wouldn't want to disappoint Angus," she said.

CHAPTER THIRTY-FOUR

Jen and I got up early, took a shower, went back to bed and made love again. Who would believe that a suggestion from a robot could be such an aphrodisiac? Carly took us to breakfast at a local diner, and then to the office for our meeting with Angus and Billy.

When we walked into the conference room, Billy and Angus were already there.

"Mike and Jenny, I must say that you two appear much more relaxed than yesterday. So does Billy. I find it fascinating how humans can rejuvenate themselves by rubbing up against one another naked."

"Thanks for your evaluation, Angus, not to mention your advice last night," Jenny said. "To change the subject, how was your night?"

"Well, I didn't get laid, if that's what you mean," Angus said, after which he laughed hysterically at his own joke. "Ayooga, ayooga, ayooga."

"I believe that I've had another breakthrough idea," Angus said after he stopped laughing. "My objective was to devise a way to inspect our products without physically removing them from their wrappings and thereby risking an explosion. I think I've come up with an electronic solution. I will send a signal to the box that contains the product and, depending on the return signal, I can tell if it's explosive or not. But we can't rely on a theory, we need to test it. My research tells me that there's a shooting range at the Suffolk County Police Headquarters where we can test my theory."

I called George Clayton, the New York City police commissioner, the guy who had approached us on finding a robotic solution to mob violence. He agreed to meet us at the local firing range along with Timothy Sini, his friend and police commissioner of Suffolk County.

Carly pulled up to the Suffolk County Police facility in Yaphank and left us at the entrance. George Clayton was there to greet us, along with Rick Bellamy from the FBI, and Suffolk Police Commissioner Sini.

The explosive test range had just been mowed, leaving behind the pleasant smell of freshly cut grass combined with gunpowder. As a safety measure, the entire field is swept with a metal and explosive detecting device before the lawn is mowed. As a further safety feature, the lawn mower is an unmanned robot, manufactured, of course, by Robot Depot.

The plan was for Angus to send an electronic signal to the various boxes we brought with us. An aide sprayed red paint on each box that Angus identified as carrying explosives. We then photographed the array of boxes. Angus aimed his remote device at each of the red painted boxes. Every one of the boxes exploded, not just with a percussive blast, but with fire spewing in all directions. As a double check, Angus sent a triggering signal to each of the boxes without red paint. Just as we expected none of them exploded. The police lab would later identify remnants of Cemtex, a powerful plastic explosive.

The electronic signal that Angus sent to the boxes came from an inexpensive remote device that could identify the explosives by just pointing and sending the signal. Angus devised the explosive detection capability.

"Well, Mike," Rick Bellamy said, "it's still going to be a gigantic recall, but it just got a lot easier. You've got to make public announcements with a huge advertising campaign to get people to call you if they own a Robot Depot device. You can give them the option of bringing the product to the local store, or we'll assign an agent, along with one of your people to go to the person's home. If the device detects explosives, we pick up the product and bring it to one of various locations to be detonated."

After the explosive range tests we returned to my office along with Rick Bellamy.

"Thanks to this robot over here, we have an excellent way to handle the recall." Bellamy said.

"Excuse me, sir, but my name is Angus, not robot."

"I'm sorry, Angus. Since my old friend Mike here got involved in robotics, I'm still learning how to be appropriate."

"I'm the only robot that is aware of itself, Mr. Bellamy, not only at Robot Depot, but probably in the entire world.

"So here's a big question for you, Angus," Bellamy said, struggling to reconcile himself with the fact that he was having a deep conversation with a machine. "Have you determined who may be the perpetrator or perpetrators?"

"My suspicion, based on all of the evidence thus far, is that Mr. Jack Winston, the quality control supervisor, is the primary suspect, but that conclusion needs to be tested against additional facts."

"But Jack Winston insisted that the tampering was an inside job from the beginning," I said. "He even fingered that guy George Livingston from his department. Remember, Livingston disappeared."

"Those facts, Mike, lead to the opposite conclusion—that Winston is innocent," Angus said. "As I pointed out, we must test my initial conclusion of his guilt against additional facts."

I almost expected Angus to say, in the spirit of Sherlock Holmes, "It's elementary my dear Watson."

"We have the dates the products were stocked on the shelves from the bar codes," Bellamy said. "Livingston disappeared a month ago. So the question is, have any products been placed on the shelves or shipped since the date Livingston disappeared? Angus?"

"No, not one. That obviously does not include products that have been shipped in the past, but it does indicate that Livingston was the last one who had anything to do with tampering before that date. What it does not explain is how Livingston could have tampered with the products while under the supervision of Winston."

Rick Bellamy and I looked at each other. We then said the same thing—Bennie.

"I want to interrogate Winston in Bennie Weinberg's presence," Bellamy said. "If Bennie-the- Bullshit-Detector sees that Winston is lying, we may have our man. I want to interview him here, where he'll be more comfortable than at the FBI office."

The idea that a man I've known and trusted for years could be the guy responsible for the disasters sickened me. I hoped Bennie could sort this shit out.

CHAPTER THIRTY-FIVE

"I don't know what the hell you guys have been waiting for," Bennie Weinberg said. "That guy Winston is the primary suspect, in my opinion. I base that opinion on simple detective reasoning, having nothing to do with psychiatry. Jack Winston is the quality control supervisor. How can somebody, Livingston or somebody else, pull off that crap without Winston's knowing it?"

Bennie, Rick Bellamy, and I were at our main manufacturing plant in Hempstead, waiting for Jack Winston to show up. Angus was in the meeting as well, along with his creator and sidekick Billy Jackson. Jenny couldn't make the meeting because she had to fly to Maryland to meet with the Army brass to go over the operating details of the *Groundhog* robots that were just delivered.

"Gentleman, Jack Winston is here," Dianne said. She showed him in.

"Mr. Winston, we've met before," said Bellamy. "As you know, our investigation into the exploding robots is a continuing one. That's why I'd like to ask you a few questions. This is my colleague Ben Weinberg. This interview will be recorded, if that's okay with you. Just to be clear, you've stated for the record that you do not choose to have an attorney present, is that correct?"

"Yes, that's correct," Winston said. "I don't need a lawyer. I want to get at the truth as much as you guys."

"Let me open our interview by making a couple of statements and asking you a rather broad question," Bellamy said. "You were the guy who pointed us to one of your employees who suddenly went missing. As quality control supervisor, how could someone tamper with any products without your knowledge? Obviously, Livingston is our main suspect at this point because he disappeared into thin air. But I'd like to know how Livingston or anybody else could tamper with a product without you knowing about it."

"I've been asking myself that same question, and I think I may have come up with an answer," Winston said. "The answer, in a word, is *solenoid*. I understand that our friend Angus here has come up with a way to detect an explosive in a packaged product. So to answer your question completely, I'm going to ask Angus to scan each product that I put on this table with his detector. My interest is in not blowing up myself and you guys with me."

I went over to a shelf and pulled the first box and put it on the table in front of Jack Winston. Angus scanned it and confirmed that it was not explosive.

"Now each product casing is opened, as is normal quality control procedure before the box is sealed." Winston said. "This happens to every single product."

Winston then casually opened the casing, ran his hand over a few parts, and closed it.

"So we need not worry about this package, right?" Winston asked all of us.

"That's right," I said, "Angus scanned it with his detector, and then you pulled it apart to inspect it further. So that package is ready to wrap and ship."

"I hate to break some explosive news, not to pun, but this package can kill all of us," Winston said.

"Ayooga, ayooga, ayooga," Angus laughed at Winston's "explosive news" pun.

"Pardon me if I'm being dense, Mr. Winston," Bellamy said, "but how can that package be explosive after it was checked out by the remote and then inspected by you personally? Am I missing something?"

"None of you noticed that I just replaced the solenoid," Winston said, "a device that's in every one of our products. A solenoid is a cylindrical coil of wire that acts as a magnet when carrying electrical current." He held up a solenoid. "The solenoid you're looking at came from the product I just examined. I removed the old solenoid and replaced it and nobody noticed. Now if I saw someone perform the task that I just did, I wouldn't have noticed it either. That's right, the quality control supervisor would not have spotted what I just did. That's because the inspector of the product is required to remove the solenoid to make sure it fits properly into its receptacle. The only difference is that I replaced it after I lifted it out. You don't need to be a circus magician to do that. You lift out one solenoid and slip in the replacement with the same hand. Now I've done some research and discovered that a solenoid can be packed with a powerful explosive. That's how soldiers place booby traps on artillery that they need to abandon. As quality control supervisor, I could follow one of my inspectors around the shop from package to package, and I never would have noticed what he did."

"So how can we possibly stop this from happening, Jack?" I asked.

"Simple, Mike. I now require each inspector to hold his hands out to the security camera so we can see if he's hiding a replacement solenoid. Also, we now scan each inspector with a metal detector before he starts his shift. Angus, am I making sense?"

"It makes perfect sense. I just searched through my database and found that a solenoid can be turned into an explosive element with a simple receiver so that it doesn't explode accidentally. It needs to be triggered by a device, either a remote signal or by use of a timing switch inside the replacement solenoid."

"Let's take a short break," Bellamy said. "Bennie and Mike, a word with you please?"

We both looked at Bennie.

"My job here today isn't to evaluate all of that engineering stuff, but to assess whether the guy telling the story is lying," Bennie said. "Well, he's not. I look at about a dozen tell-tale signals of lying such as perspiration, eye movements, speech patterns, and general demeanor. There's not a hint that this guy Winston is lying. If he gave me the name of a horse, I'd bet on it. Besides that, although this part isn't my job, I found his engineering explanation to be credible as hell. This guy deserves a big raise, not an arrest warrant."

Jack Winston returned from the break.

"Mr. Winston, we thank you for your straightforward answers during our interview before the break," Bellamy said. "I just want to ask you some questions about the other exploding robot cases. We know about the explosions at the private homes, including Mike's house, because you and Angus have pretty much covered those. But what about the Jameston Building in Chicago? All of the robots congregated on one floor. Your thoughts on that?"

"There's no sense having a robot if you can't tell it what to do and where to go," Winston said. "The problem with the Jameston bots was the same as we've discussed today—they were rigged to explode on signal, and somebody commandeered the device that sends orders to the robots. The problem with their all going to the same place was not a problem, just a useful and normal robotic function for the killers to take advantage of, which they did. The bots simply went where they were told to go."

"And how about the exploding drones at Yankee stadium, where Mike, Bennie and Mike's wife were almost blown up?" Bellamy asked.

"A drone is a different story. Once you have a drone in your possession, you can tamper with it to your heart's content. They probably bought those drones at various Robot Depot locations around the country or online. Think of them like guns. Once you buy one, the manufacturer can't control what you do with it. The same thing with the erratic robots on that cruise ship. Anybody can tamper with a product once it's out of the wrapper."

"So we're left with a primary suspect, George Livingston, but we don't know where he is," I said, "and we have no idea about the scumbags who attacked Yankee stadium."

"So let me summarize where we are, and if anybody has any input please let's hear it," Bellamy said. "I think our exploding robot problem will soon be over except for the few out there who don't answer the recall. Between your brilliant quality control supervisor and your amazing colleague, Angus, you seem to have that problem under control. Mike, I think you should could go on national TV with your big recall, and I don't mean just an ad, but nationally televised news programs. I don't know how you can convince TV executives to do that."

"No problem with national news outlets, Rick. Our PR lady, Blanche Whiteacre, can get me an audience with the Pope if she wanted to."

"Any other thoughts?" Bellamy asked.

"Drones are the big problem as I see it, Rick," I said. "Yes, any exploding robots whose owners never get the message can be a problem, but it's limited. I hate the idea of government regulation, but I sure as hell wouldn't mind seeing some kind of restrictions on people buying drones. And that problem isn't limited to Robot Depot. Shit, you can go to a local store and buy a flying drone from various manufacturers and fly it wherever you want, carrying whatever will fit, as long as you keep the thing under the FAA limit of 400 feet. If Jeff Bezos thinks he can deliver Amazon goods to a person's doorstep, what can a terrorist do?"

"My gut tells me we haven't seen anything yet," Bennie Weinberg said, "and that's no bullshit."

CHAPTER THIRTY-SIX

"A terror spectacular, in answer to the question you're about to ask me," Jenny said.

She had just returned from her meeting with the Army people in Maryland. I told her all about our meeting with Jack Winston, and our conclusion that he's not one of the bad guys. I was about to ask her what her major concern was. As usual she anticipated my question and answered it.

"Right as usual, Jen. I was about to ask you what you think is the biggest problem we're facing."

"Mike, name some terror spectaculars, I mean big attacks that grab the world's attention,"

"Well, I'll begin with 9/11, then the Boston Marathon bombing, the Paris shootings, the Jameston Building, which involved our stuff, and the Yankee Stadium drone attacks, which also involved our products. What do you think?"

"What worries the hell out of me," Jenny said, "is a terror spectacular that consists of thousands of little attacks, just like in guerilla warfare. With all of the crap that's happened in the last few weeks, I think we're right in the middle of a terror spectacular now. The house fires caused by our exploding bots come to mind. But what about a single actor, not necessarily a suicide bomber, who gets his hands on destructive devices that, when added together, result in one huge terror event. We've seen hints of it, with simultaneous bombings of trains in one city, or the multiple attacks in Paris. Imagine a bunch of terrorists who buy our floor cleaning bots. Even after the new quality control procedures that Jack Winston talked about at your meeting, nothing prevents a terrorist from going out, weaponizing a single bot, and turning it loose. Say a hundred scumbags do this in a hundred different cities. Now that's a terror spectacular that's easy to plan and easy to execute because the spectacular event involves a whole bunch of single attacks. Hey, we saw what happened to Yankee stadium. That was a carefully planned flight with hundreds of drones. What about simultaneous attacks on different stadiums all over the country. It would tie up news reports for weeks besides killing a lot of people."

"So what's your thinking, hon?" I said. "You're talking about events that are almost impossible to prevent, at least not on the scale you're thinking about. Law enforcement has gotten pretty good at preventing big attacks, pretty good but not perfect. Think Yankee Stadium. But how the hell does law enforcement stop one guy, whose only contact with a central authority is that he was given a date, a time, and a place? How can you prevent something like that, the proverbial lone wolf?"

"My thinking is that law enforcement, including the FBI and the CIA needs to infiltrate more than they are already," Jenny said. "If you know about something in advance, you can stop it, but you've got to know about it. We've been looking at this problem as if it's unique to Robot Depot. What about selective poisoning of local food supplies, or poisoning a fresh water reservoir? No robots involved there. I'd like to share my thoughts with Rick Bellamy, although I'm sure he's ahead of me on this. It's just that big stuff tends to crowd out small stuff."

"What you're saying sounds like the beginning of a third world war," I said.

"That's an accurate way of putting it Mike. Nobody's named it yet, but I think we're already fighting World War III."

CHAPTER THIRTY-SEVEN

"How many?" I asked.

"Five," Blanche replied.

"Have I told you recently how amazing you are, Blanche? Three days ago I asked you to set me up on major TV news shows, and already you've gotten me five placements."

"I just give the producer a stake in the interview, Mike. I didn't entice them with the CEO of a company who wants to make apologies for broken products. I emphasized that it's a national emergency involving terrorism. The average time for a producer to get back to me was 10 minutes. I booked you with two Sunday morning shows, Neil Cavuto again for tomorrow afternoon, Wolf Blitzer for the next day, and—get this—Lara Logan wants you back on *60 Minutes* for this coming Sunday. She wants to tape you on Thursday. We don't want to duck the fact that the products involved were from Robot Depot, because the obvious purpose of the recall is to get people to have their robots checked out. You need to emphasize that terrorism is the reason for the bombings. People hate terrorism. It's our job to show the world that Robot

Depot a victim too. So you have three basic themes, the product re-call, our new quality control, and that fact that we're victims along with everybody else."

"What about drones, Blanche? They're the big problem in the future, and there's little we can do about it."

"But we're not the only drone manufacturer."

"No, we're not, but we are the biggest. I should emphasize that the drones that leave our facility are safe, but if a scumbag wants to put a bomb in one we can't control the result."

"Great, but maybe don't refer to the bad guys as scumbags," Blanche said.

"I think I should do a visual demonstration of how we in-spect the robots as Jack Winston showed us. People will see that it was almost impossible for an inspection supervisor to see what happened."

"God, no, unless you're asked," Blanche said. "Visuals tend to stick with people. We don't want to put a thought in their heads that Robot Depot is really Bomb Depot. Just explain how even an experienced supervisor did not see the piece being replaced. Now remember, these people are journalists and it's their job to drill down and get to the facts. Yes, some of them will try to paint you as a bad guy, but most will ask questions that beg to be answered. Mike, I've seen you in action on TV so many times that I know you're a cool cucumber under pressure, except when you wore that stupid fucking robot costume on that commercial. Your job is to be yourself and explain what happened, what we're doing about it, and to make sure they call the 800 number if they own one of the suspect robots. And I want other executives to appear on TV, not just you, just like I did with Shepard Smith. I want to avoid a time when people turn on the TV and see your face and say, 'Oh shit, what now?' "

"We've even come up with a partial solution to the drone prob-lem," I said. "pretty lame if you ask me, but it's something. We're going to require photographic identification, such as a driver's license, to buy a drone. Of course the innocent buyer of a drone has nothing to worry about. Requiring a photo ID shows that we're diligent. The law doesn't require it but we will."

"Mike, it's going to take a lot more than showing that we're diligent. You've got to show the world that Robot Depot is a force for good, and that's why the bad guys are after us."

CHAPTER THIRTY-EIGHT

"Yankee Stadium was a wonderful success, my brothers," Farouk Mahmood said. "You showed how the wings of death can swoop down on the infidels without warning and cause enormous destruction."

Farouk Mahmood, one of the most powerful leaders of ISIS, was meeting with the two men responsible for the drone attacks on Yankee Stadium. They met at an ISIS "safe house" in Fairfield, Connecticut. Ali Mujahedeen, his chief lieutenant was also at the meeting.

"Ali, I don't believe you've met these two brothers before, Walter Buono and James Flager. They are known by their infidel names on my orders. I am pleased to introduce my most trusted advisor and operative, Sheik George Livingston, better known among us as Ali Mujahedeen. His work as an insider at Robot Depot made all of the attacks we've discussed possible. "

"The timing of the event could not have been better," Livingston said, a 'Subway Series' between New York's two professional base-ball teams. I must also commend you on your choice of locations for the drones prior to the attack. Ten different launch sites meant that the mission became a success before anyone noticed. With every action like the one you two carried out, the infidel cringes before the Islamic State."

"The past two months have given us much reason to praise Allah and the good fortune he has bestowed on us," Mahmood said, "and one company, Robot Depot, has provided us with the weapons of destruction. Since Brother Livingston infiltrated the company we've seen vast destruction caused by bomb carrying robots, from private house fires, to the destruction of the Jameston Building in Chicago, to the chaos aboard that cruise ship, to the drone attack at Yankee Stadium. The infidel is learning to tremble before us."

"Perhaps you should share with our young brothers here what you told me before," Livingston said to Farouk Mahmood.

"What Ali is talking about, brothers, are our plans for the future. It is critically important that we lurk in the shadows and do not call attention to ourselves. You two have taken your Western names, which is good, but we must also be careful with our conversations, and especially never to speak in Arabic. All of us need to become a part of the scenery and not stand out. We will become invisible so that we may kill the infidels with the explosions and fires of hell. Our insiders tell us that there are 877 private houses in the country that contain explosive robots. We are working on plans to fly drones over the houses and detonate the devices with a signal as we've done in the past. Our objective is to create as many explosions as near in time as possible in order to create chaos."

"Sheik Mahmood, can you tell us about any plans that may be in the works for attacking the robotics in driverless cars?" Said Jim Flager, one of the Yankee Stadium attackers.

"We are waiting for a critical mass of such vehicles to take to the roads. We don't want to tip our hands and give the infidel time to create countermeasures. Our current plan calls for attacks on driverless cars when 10,000 of them are on the road, not just as experiments, but in operation as private vehicles and cars for hire. Our studies tell us that the competition is heating up for manufacturers and users such as Uber. That company will save a fortune when it doesn't need to pay its thousands of drivers. We will see to it that there are not only driverless vehicles but wrecked vehicles. Once we've placed enough explosive robotic devices in a large number of cars, we can cause chaos at rush hour in major cities when suddenly out-of-control robot cars slam into regular cars and trucks."

"The sacred caliphate will soon be upon us, thanks to your leadership, Sheik Mahmood," Buono said. "And thanks also to the bravery of Brother Livingston."

"I caution you, my brothers," Mahmood said, "do not ever use the infidel name George Livingston. Brother Ali Mujahedeen works for the praise of Allah in the shadows, as do we all, the *Shadows of Terror*."

CHAPTER THIRTY-NINE

"Good evening, ladies and gentlemen, I'm Lara Logan for *60 Minutes*, reporting from the corporate offices of the automation giant, Robot Depot. A few weeks ago we taped a segment at one of the Robot Depot stores where I interviewed Mike Bateman, CEO and founder of the company. Mr. Bateman took us on a narrative tour of the modern world of robotics and artificial intelligence. Mr. Bateman disputed the claims of many who find that robotics and AI are responsible for a huge change in the American job economy, especially the disappearance of blue collar jobs like cab driving, truck driving, and food service positions across many fast food outlets the world over. Mr. Bateman, or Mike as he prefers to be called, gave us a different picture, one of optimism."

As was prearranged, Joe, the coffee bot wheeled up to Lara Logan with a tray of coffee.

"Thank you, Joe," Lara said.

"Mike is in favor of guaranteed jobs to replace entry level and manual labor with a host of exciting ideas for the future," Logan continued. "To listen to Mike, you felt confident that Robot Depot is a force for good, not a job-slaying dragon as many have suggested. Their most exciting recent invention is an artificial intelligence medical database that diagnoses just about any disease or syndrome imaginable. At a recent presentation at Columbia Presbyterian Medical Center, a Robot Depot artificial intelligence robot named Angus was pitted against 150 physicians in a contest to see who could accurately diagnose 17 real medical cases. Angus correctly diagnosed all 17, including five cases that had resulted in death. Angus took 15 seconds to read the symptoms and background of each patient, compared to eight and a half minutes for the human doctors, and he didn't make a single mistake.

"But the picture isn't entirely bright, and it's got nothing to do with Mike Bateman. The world of terrorism has discovered Robot Depot, and the results are staggering. In a matter of weeks Robot Depot machines have been implicated in six house fires, including the Batemans's own home, a crippled cruise ship, the destruction of the Jameston Building in Chicago, and the horrific attack on the Yankees-Mets game at Yankee Stadium. We asked Mike Bateman to join us again, along with his wife Jenny Bateman, the company's Vice President for Product Development.

"Mike, please give us your reaction to the horrible scenes of violence that have involved your company's products."

"In a word, Lara, sabotage, and we believe it's terrorism. A man who worked in our quality control department suddenly disappeared. Not only did he disappear, but an FBI agent who went to his house to execute a search warrant, was blown up after he stepped on a booby trap. I can't speak for law enforcement, but as of now we have no idea where the saboteur went."

"Mike, please tell us more about quality control at Robot Depot," Logan said. "People are questioning how a quality control procedure could enable robots to leave the plant with bombs attached. How could that happen?"

I told Lara Logan and the *60 Minutes* audience all about our quality control and how the vice president in charge showed us how to replace a solenoid with an exploding one, and none of us, including agents from the FBI and CIA, even noticed what he did. The interview was positive, I thought. Logan is a good journalist and a serious one, not a reporter who loves to play "gotcha." She asked Jenny about new product development, and Jen, as I knew she would, did a great job of answering her questions.

"Ladies and gentleman, I'm glad that we invited Mike and Jenny Bateman to appear on *60 Minutes* this evening. It's shocking, from everything we've heard from the Batemans, as well as a representative of the FBI, what is happening to this fine company. Some terrorist group sees Robot Depot, not as an innovative forward-looking company that does a lot of good in the world, but as a supplier of explosive delivery machines."

Blanche waited for us when we finished the *60 Minutes* taping. She had been standing to the side and saw the entire segment. I waved her over to meet Lara Logan. After three minutes of chatting, Blanche and Lara acted like life-long girlfriends.

"You two are fabulous," she said after the CBS crew left. "I think we should change the name of Robot Depot to the *Mike and Jenny Show*. Anyone watching should be convinced that the terror bullshit has nothing to do with us. That gal Lara is a doll, and she's no stranger to terrorists. I remember that she was attacked and molested by a bunch of thugs in Egypt a few years ago. Okay, Mike, the Cavuto show is tomorrow. Go home and get some rest."

⊷⊶

The Cavuto show went as well as *60 Minutes*. Neil Cavuto, like Lara Logan, is a real pro. Of course they'd deny it, but I had a feeling they were cheering me on. Inevitably, one morning show was an explosion of negativity. *The Max Cornell Show* is conducted by its namesake, Max Cornell, an aging leftist who relishes the opportunity to "speak truth to power," as he loves to say. The theme of the show was that he was the truth, and I was the power. If his viewers listened carefully, they would think that I personally inserted the bombs into the exploding bots. Fortunately he has very few viewers. Blanche did not set me up for that show. Cornell's producer called and I agreed to appear, a dumb move on my part. I should know to clear stuff like this with Blanche, as she loudly suggested to me after the *Cornell* show.

Our public relations campaign was going well, we all agreed—except for the *Max Cornell Show*. I think I was doing a decent job of convincing viewers that Robot Depot had been sabotaged, and that we really are good guys. Well, shit, we are. One of the reasons for the success of my road show was that there had been no bombings or any other crazy bot events in over two weeks. How long can that last? I wondered.

CHAPTER FORTY

"This is the biggest children's regatta I've ever seen, Phil," said Toby Plimpton, the commodore of the North Fork Sailing Club in Southold, Long Island.

"You got that right, Toby," said his friend Phil Jamison, the vice commodore. "I counted 125 boats on moorings and the regatta isn't until tomorrow."

The event they spoke about is the annual Windy Boats regatta for kids up to age 15. The race would begin in Southold Bay, continue out to Peconic Bay toward Gardiner's Bay and Plum Island, and then return to the starting line in Southold Bay. The kids' sailboats would be tailed by adults in powerboats, which would serve as committee boats to enforce the rules, as well as act as safety boats in case a sail boat capsized. The regatta was scheduled to begin the next day at 11 a.m. The mid-July weather called for calm seas, ideal for sailboat racing. It would be a "one design" race, where all of the boats are of similar size and design. The light wind favored the kids with the best sailing skills.

The committeeman with starter pistol saw the typical jam-up of boats jockeying for good position to cross the starting line as soon as the gun fired. Within an hour, the major part of the fleet rounded Shelter Island, some far ahead, others way behind.

Toby Plimpton and Phil Jamison motored at a slight distance from the fleet in Plimpton's 25-foot Steigercraft powerboat. They kept as far away from the sailboats as possible to avoid interfering with the kids' ability to maneuver.

"What's that noise?" Phil asked, looking up.

"It sounds like a bunch of pissed off bees," Toby said.

"Holy shit, look at that," Jamison said, pointing to a flight of over 200 foot-wide helicopter drones. "It looks like we're not the only ones hosting a race."

"Yeah, but they seem to be in formation, not racing each other."

The drones dropped in altitude and then started to dive at the boats. In moments, the sight and sound of explosions ripped through the regatta. Masts fell, sails shredded, and boats crashed into one another.

"Everybody get into the water," Toby screamed into his megaphone. Since the rules required that everyone wear a life jacket, he figured it was a lot safer in the water then on the boats that for some crazy reason had become targets. He maneuvered his Steigercraft slowly, as did the other powerboats, so as not to hit a kid in the water. Every committee boat captain hailed the Coast Guard with a mayday emergency alert. Within minutes there were no more drones aloft. Two Coast Guard Sea King helicopters came into view with ladders lowered and a Coast Guardsman on the lower rung, aided by divers in scuba gear maneuvering a stretcher to help pick up young sailors in the water. Besides shattered boats and sails all over the bay, the Coast Guardsmen could see floating bodies.

Toby Plimpton's Steigercraft was one of the last boats hit. The drone flew into the opening and crashed into the steering console where Plimpton and Jamison stood, killing them both in the ensuing explosion.

"What the fuck is going on?" shouted News 12 TV Reporter, Jack Duncan, into the camera, not paying attention to his language. He and his cameraman stood on the shore to avoid turbulence when taping the race. He looked into the camera, tears streaming down his face.

"Ladies and gentlemen," his voice choking as he spoke, "the past five minutes were the most brutal that I've seen since Vietnam. It's even worse than a war zone. These kids were attacked by God knows who for God knows what reason. We don't like to speculate about terrorism, but what kind of twisted demon would do this to a bunch of children?"

The small section of Long Island suddenly became a worldwide news event. A reporter from Los Angeles who used to live in Southold asked the News 12 reporter if he could speak to his old friend, Toby Plimpton. The *News 12* guy went off the air for a few moments and told him that he just saw Plimpton's body dragged ashore and put into a body bag.

Walter Bowman, the Supervisor of Southold Town, was on the air, a man known for his blunt language. His face told of the feelings he was about to express. "I am going to hunt down and kill the scumbags who did this," he said, after which he broke down in tears.

The local *News 12* reporter continued what he thought would be a pleasant news assignment, providing as much detail as he could put together, which wasn't much. A high aerial view over Peconic Bay said it all—a beautiful bay, littered with sails, smashed up boats, and young bodies.

⟞⟊ ⟊⟝

I picked up the phone, interrupting my TV viewing of the horrible scene on Peconic Bay. It was Tom Logan, a Robot Depot executive calling from his vacation home in Southold.

"They're ours, Mike. I looked at two of them that were duds. I just wanted to let you know I'm coming back to the office."

"Tommy, you're on vacation," I said. "Just try to relax. There isn't much you can do about the situation here."

"Mike, the last fucking place in the world I want to be right now is beautiful Southold Town. I can see the debris and bodies from my deck."

⋙⋘

"Rick, it's Mike Bateman. I just got a call, and it looks like the drones are ours."

"Please be at my office at 9 a.m. tomorrow," said Bellamy. "I'm going to put some stuff in motion."

Bellamy continued to stare at the TV after he hung up with Bateman.

It's time to go to war, he thought.

CHAPTER FORTY-ONE

B ennie Weinberg walked into Rick Bellamy's office at 26 Federal Plaza for a meeting with Rick Bellamy and me.

"Yankee Stadium really screwed with my head for a few days," Bennie said, "especially because I was there. But this satanic regatta attack takes the fucking cake. Who would launch an attack that targeted children? I think we're dealing with a new sub-species of human being, a species where all of the members are psychopaths."

"I think you're right, Ben" Bellamy said. "We're seeing a new level of depravity. That's what convinced me to go on offense. Of course what I'm about to say doesn't leave this room, but I just got a wink and a nod from 1600 Pennsylvania Avenue."

"An Agent Atkins is here to see you, Mr. Bellamy," his assistant said.

A tall Middle Eastern looking guy walked in. Both Bennie and Rick Bellamy stood to greet him as if he were an old fraternity brother. Rick then introduced him to me.

"Please call me Buster, everyone else does. I don't know if Rick or Bennie told you, but I'm with the CIA. A lot of people look at me as if I just rode in on a camel. I'm a Coptic Christian, and I get my looks from my Egyptian parents who also taught me to speak fluent Arabic. Some people say that I'm a jihadi's worst nightmare—I look like them, but I'm *not* one of them."

"I guess Rick brought you up to speed about what's going on with Robot Depot," I said. "Some group has narrowed down their choice of weapons to our inventory. The problem started with exploding robotic floor cleaners. The big problem now is with our helicopter drones, the kind that attacked Yankee Stadium and that children's regatta. We're also concerned about robots that we've sold over the past three years that may contain explosive devices. We've figured out that the explosives on the robots were inserted in-house, and we're sure we've minimized the problem with a huge public relations recall campaign, but that doesn't address the aerial drone problem. Anybody can buy a drone, from us or another store, and weaponize the goddam thing with explosives. That's what happened at Yankee Stadium and at the children's regatta on Long Island."

"One of your quality control people was named George Livingston, I understand, and he suddenly disappeared, yes?"

"Yes, you've done your homework, Buster," I said.

"Livingston's Muslim name is Ali Mujahedeen and he currently resides in Yemen," Buster said. "He's now back in the States as of last Tuesday."

Bennie, Rick, and myself all said variations of "holy shit."

"We don't call Buster Mr. Super Spook for nothing," Bellamy said.

"I can't go into more detail than that, I'm sure you understand," Buster said. "But be happy knowing that we have that cockroach under tight surveillance while we wait for his next move. When he takes his next action we'll either capture him or kill him. Livingston, or Mujahedeen, has been a major player in infiltrating and sabotaging Robot Depot and its products. Our surveillance of him has given us the identities of three other people, one of whom we think is a member of senior ISIS management."

"Buster is the team leader for this operation," Bellamy said, "and I'm his deputy. Those orders came right from the White House to the Department of Defense, to the FBI and CIA commands. Buster and I have worked many a case together, and I think he's the best in the business, including both the FBI and the CIA. I'm happy to work with him."

"For the first time in a long while," I said, "I feel a bit optimistic that we can defeat those animals."

"I appreciate your confidence in us, Mike, but it isn't going to be easy," Buster said. "ISIS thinks that it's found the perfect manufacturer of bomb carrying devices through your company. By the way, do drones account for a large part of your sales?"

"Yes," I said. "Drones account for about eight percent of our revenue."

"Well, just to give you a heads up, my friend," Buster said, "the government is about to announce a moratorium on all drone sales from any outlet in the country. Shortly we'll see a bill come out of the House of Representatives that will require strict licensing procedures before anybody can buy a drone. Until that bill passes, the moratorium will remain in effect. I hope I haven't ruined your day, Mike."

"No, Buster, you haven't," I said. "Drones are wonderful devices, but so are guns and bombs if used by the right people. I've always found it crazy that anybody can walk in off the street and buy a drone, strap an explosive device to it, and blow something up. Robot Depot is just one component of the drone manufacturing and sales industry, but we're the biggest. The industry will lobby like mad against that bill, but Robot Depot won't be a part of the opposition. Actually we're going to enthusiastically support the legislation. I normally hate government regulation, but in this case it's needed."

"From what I've been told about you, Mike, you just said what I expected to hear," Buster said. "It's an honor to know you."

"Buster and I are going to go into committee now and work on some details," Rick Bellamy said. "Ben, Mike, I trust you guys completely, but the 'need to know' doctrine tells us that we can't share all information with you. Your thoughts, Buster?"

"Let's go kill some rats."

CHAPTER FORTY-TWO

"I think I know who you've got in mind, Buster," Rick Bellamy said, "and I'll bet his name begins with 'Imam.' "

"The one and only, Rick, Mr. Insider himself, a born spook and the best mole we have."

Mike, aka Muhammed Busharif, is the imam of a mosque in Brooklyn. Mike is six feet tall with the physique of a body builder, which he was for many years. He has to explain constantly to people in his mosque why he doesn't wear a beard. He blames it on a rare skin condition. Truth is, Mike simply didn't like beards. For most of his religious career, he quietly tended to the flock that worshipped at his mosque. But over time he became infuriated with all of the terrorist killings in the name of his religion. When a good friend of his daughter was killed in a bomb attack at a football game, Mike went over the edge. He's renounced his religion, but only to a select few people. Mike's language tends to be profane, not what you'd expect from a religious leader. Mike is the most important mole the CIA ever had, and feeds them information they could never get without an insider like him. In his mosque, Mike hears things that wouldn't faze a non-clergyman. Mike is also famous among the select few agents from the CIA and a couple from the FBI for his disguises.

"Let me guess that you want us to meet Mike at the Loeb Boathouse restaurant in Central Park," Bellamy said. "I think that you volunteer to come to New York just to go there."

"Okay, I'll admit it's my favorite place, perfect for a meeting," Buster said. "CIA Director Carlini calls the place 'Buster's Boathouse.' I'll call Imam Mike and arrange for lunch tomorrow."

"I can't wait to see his latest disguise," Bellamy said.

CHAPTER FORTY-THREE

Buster and Rick sat at a table on the outside of the Loeb Boathouse overlooking the lake. Buster preferred outside tables on the lake because exterior seats provided the best privacy. It was a warm July day, with a temperature of 85 degrees, but comfortable humidity.

As they perused the menu, a Catholic nun walked up to their table. She wore a full habit of the Dominican Order.

"Looks like we're about to be solicited for a donation to something," Bellamy said.

"I hope you two fuckers said grace before meals," Imam Mike said.

They both cracked up, Bellamy squirting club soda through both nostrils.

"Please have a seat, sister," Buster said. "It must be hot for you to wear a full habit in this heat."

"Not a problem. I wear shorts and a tee shirt underneath."

"It's great to see you again, Mike," Bellamy said.

"It's good to see you too, Rick. Please congratulate your wife Ellen. I read that she won another architectural award. She's a hell of a talented lady."

"Thanks, Mike," Bellamy said. "It doesn't surprise me that you knew about her award. You don't seem to miss anything."

"Mike, I'm guessing that you know what we want to talk about," Buster said.

"Let me see," Mike said. "Could it be something to do with exploding robots and drones? What else is there to talk about over the past month? That big company, Robot Depot, seems to be involved in the majority of robot attacks, correct?"

"Yes, we think it's because Robot Depot is the biggest manufacturer of robots and drones," Bellamy said.

"There's more to it than just a supply of bomb-carrying machines," Mike pointed out. "Let me tell you a story that I heard two days ago. It will blow your minds. Mike Bateman, the founder and CEO of Robot Depot, served as a Marine captain in Afghanistan before he turned his mind to business. Two guys in my mosque were talking about just that, and not only Bateman's heroics, but of a particular incident in a small village. Bateman led a platoon of Marines to capture the village, because it was a steady supplier of jihadis who killed Bateman's men on a regular basis. The guy in my mosque said that he personally saw Bateman gun down three men, two of whom were the guy's brothers and the third was his father. A woman, wearing a full burqa and armed with an AK-47, charged at Bateman. He shot her too. The woman was the mother of the guy in my mosque. So in one incident, Mike Bateman wiped out this guy's entire family. And guess what? The guy's looking for payback, and he's already collected a lot of it. It's obvious, to me anyway, that they're looking to destroy Bateman's company. But I know these types, and so do you. The guy won't be happy until he kills Bateman, probably by himself."

"Do you know his full name?" Buster asked.

"Farouk Mahmood. Sound familiar?"

"Holy shit," said Buster. "He's senior management with ISIS. I didn't know he was in the States."

"I just learned the guy's full identity. He's been in the States for about two months," Mike said. "He's a regular at my mosque. I was about to call you to give you an update when you called me."

"Mike, this is unbelievably great information," Buster said.

"Do you recall hearing the name George Livingston, aka Ali Mujahedeen?" Bellamy asked.

"Yes, he's the guy that Mahmood was speaking to. I think he's Mahmood's chief aide. I didn't know that he was also known as George Livingston, but I have heard that name mentioned," Mike said. "I recall Mahmood saying that Mujahedeen had done a wonderful job. I remember you saying that he's in Yemen, but obviously he's back in the States."

"Now we have to figure out how to nail these guys without blowing Imam Mike's cover." Buster said, softly.

"Do you guys think I'm an amateur? Here are their home addresses. One in Brooklyn and one in Queens. Just don't tell them I sent you."

"Sister, as usual you've been great," Buster said. "Can I buy you another beer?"

CHAPTER FORTY-FOUR

"I'm going to the office early, Jen. You stay here and relax for a while. You didn't seem to sleep well last night."

"Have I told you how much I love you recently?" Jen said.

"You can never say it too much, and neither can I. I love you, babe."

Being married to Mike Bateman is never boring. He's a never-ending stream of fascinating ideas. I love that I decided to leave the university and work full time at Robot Depot. It's more fun, and I get to see a lot more of Mike. Sounds strange coming from a woman who's been married to the same guy for over 10 years, but it's true. I love being near him, and I thinks he's happy to have me around, even with my occasionally foul mouth. Tomorrow we're taking off early and going to our lake house in the Adirondacks. But there's something about the solitude of being on the lake that calms us down, and after all of the shit that's been happening, we need to be calmed down.

After we kissed goodbye I went upstairs, took a shower and got dressed. I went back to the kitchen to pour myself another cup of coffee. As I glanced out the window I saw that Carly was still parked there. Where the hell is Mike? I wondered. I poured my coffee and walked outside. The humidity was starting to percolate, with the temperature already 85 degrees at 8 a.m. I immediately noticed that Mike wasn't in the driver's seat, where he usually sits even though Carly does the driving. I walked up to the passenger door and dropped my coffee mug to the pavement. Mike, partially decapitated, was slumped across the seat. His head was twisted toward the window, as if he wanted to speak to me. His eyes were wide open, staring at nothing. The interior front of the car was drenched in his blood.

That instant, that morning, that entire fucking day—I've tried to rinse all of it out of my mind. I didn't want to remember what I saw. It was as if my life was reduced to that one scene of Mike's slaughtered body. Bennie Weinberg, a great guy, told me constantly in the months after Mike died, that I shouldn't try to force the scene out of my mind, that I should let it in and time itself would take care of the pain. But it wasn't happening. Mike, *my* Mike, was dead—and whoever killed him was alive.

The board of directors unanimously chose me as the new CEO of Robot Depot. I took the job, not only as a way to keep busy and to occupy my still-grieving mind, but I felt that it would keep me closer to Mike's memory. Also, because revenues were way down as a result of the exploding robots and drones, the treasury of Robot Depot wasn't in a position to entice a hotshot chief executive with a multi-million dollar deal. They offered me $1.5 million a year, nowhere near as much as Mike used to make, but I'm not Mike. I accepted the offer.

I didn't put our house on the market, even though it's far too big for just one person. We rebuilt it after the fire, and it looks as it always did. Something about the place soothes me. I think it's my memories of Mike. Every room reminded me of him, and somehow I found that strangely comforting. I did get rid of Carly. No fucking way in hell could I ever sit in that car after seeing Mike's dead body and blood all over the seats.

I sat in on a meeting with Rick Bellamy, Bennie Weinberg, and that guy from the CIA they call Buster. I can't imagine a sharper bunch of guys. They welcomed me into their circle as they had done with Mike. They knew that I didn't have much more information to give them. What they didn't know is that *I* wanted information from them. I wanted names, which I knew they had, addresses, and places of work. I knew the name of Farouk Mahmood, the man whose family Mike shot in Afghanistan. They told Mike that Mahmood now resided in the States, and Mike told me. They also said that the treasonous scumbag Livingston had returned to the States from his home in Yemen. I learned that his other name was Ali Mujahedeen. We kept little from each other over the years. But Mike's dead—and Mahmood and Livingston are alive. From my study of Islamic culture and the "Religion of Peace," I surmised that Mahmood himself butchered Mike, *my* Mike.

So Farouk Mahmood and George Livingston are not only alive, but they live in the United States.

CHAPTER FORTY-FIVE

Besides keeping busy running Robot Depot, I spent at least three evenings a week at a local shooting range. I was already a good shot, as I learned in the Marines, but I wanted to keep up my weapons proficiency, including the use of an AR-15. I learned how to handle a knife at a local martial arts studio. I also kept up my proficiency in karate, in which I held a brown belt. Can't be too careful.

Mike's been gone for two months, but the passage of time isn't working its magic the way it's supposed to. One of the rituals of our marriage was morning coffee. Mike, always an early riser, would be in the kitchen making coffee before I came down to join him for our first cup.

"Good morning, honey," I would invariably say. Yes, it was a ritual, one of those repetitive things you do or say because it feels so natural.

Today I would preside over my first board meeting at Robot Depot. I woke up early, showered, walked into the kitchen, and said, "Good morning, honey." I said that. This morning. Two months after Mike was killed.

"Good morning to you too, hon," my sister Meghan said. Meg had just gone through a nasty divorce from a violent, drunk son-of-a-bitch. Although Meg pulled in a large salary as a chemist with a big chemical manufacturing company, her asshole of a spouse managed to gamble away their entire investment account and left them deeply in debt. Because she had foolishly cosigned a bunch of the loans, Meg was on the hook for the debts. Meg and I always got along great, although during her five years of marriage to the drunk prick we didn't see each other much. She's a year younger than me, and recently turned 35. After Mike's death, Meg was at my side during the worst period of my life. Meg and Blanche, who had become my second sister, were my support group. They both asked why I had chosen to stay in the house after Mike was killed. The place is huge, with two entirely separate wings in addition to the master wing. After the fire we restored it to its original layout. Mike and I put the space to use when entertaining guests from out of town. I convinced Meg to move in and I insisted that she not pay rent. I wanted to help her get back on her financial legs after her divorce. Fortunately they didn't have any kids, and, thanks to Mike, I'm loaded with money.

Meg took off early to drive to her job in Mineola, about 30 miles away. "Roady," my replacement robotic car after I got rid of Carly, pulled up to the front of the house under the porte-cochere, a design element that Mike insisted on, replicating the one on the home office that I recommended. It was pouring rain, making me happy we agreed on the porte-cochere. But it made me think of Mike, which started me crying again. Two months, two fucking months without the love of my life. Suck it up, I said to myself. You've got a board meeting to run. Besides CEO, Mike was also chairman of the 20-member board of directors of Robot Depot. The board members were impressed with my Yale MBA and my activities at the company so they offered me the board chairman-ship as well. They were also impressed with the fact that I was the company's largest shareholder. As I learned in business school, "Don't fuck with the majority owner."

One of the members of the board was a minister, and he asked us to bow our heads in memory of Mike. I thought that was a nice gesture. I also pondered that there's another group of people who are going to need prayers, and soon.

We then heard the treasurer's report from Scotty Trumball, the board treasurer. It wasn't good news. Our sales had started to drop months before Mike's death because of the countless explod-ing robot stories, stories that were true. Sales of aerial drones had once been our largest source of revenue, but drone sales died to a trickle after Yankee Stadium and the regatta attack, and then the government announced a moratorium on the sale of aerial drones.

"Jenny, I'm really worried about our drone sales, not to mention our floor cleaning robots," said board member Susan Tampini, a local bank president with a sharp eye for reading financial state-ments. "Whoever these terrorists are, we don't seem to be able to resist their attacks. Hell, they even killed your wonderful husband. Do you have any information from the FBI that you're able to share with us?"

"Susan, and everybody," I said, "that's a critical question. I can tell you this. From my meetings with the FBI as well as the CIA, I have full confidence that the terrorist problem is going to improve, if not go away. The government investigators impress the hell out of me, and soon we're going to see people going to jail. (*Those who aren't killed, of course.*) This is the end of September. I predict that our terror problems will be over before the New Year."

The meeting ended. Each board member walked up to me and shook my hand, congratulating me on the first meeting, and thanking me for the encouraging news about the terrorists.

Yes, I thought. Our terrorist problem will soon go away.

CHAPTER FORTY-SIX

Meg and I met for dinner at Mario's in Hauppauge, a place that Mike and I frequented. I've been seeing Bennie Weinberg, the detective shrink, for informal psychotherapy. He kept emphasizing that I shouldn't try to push my thoughts about Mike out of my head. Don't bury your memories, he would say. Face them and don't try to force them out of your mind. Those savages may have killed my husband, but they're not going to control me.

I talked to Meg about chemistry, telling her that Robot Depot was thinking of developing a new robotic farming machine, one that can lay down pesticides. Meg does a lot of her work in pesticides. Agribusiness is among the many areas I'm thinking about expanding into.

"Suffolk County is the number one agricultural county in New York State," I said. "I'm thinking about some heavy duty pesticides, Meg. What's the nastiest one on the market?"

"There's a new chemical on the market with the brand name 'Cropinsure,' " Meg said. "Used properly with safety procedures and protective clothing, it's great stuff. But it's dangerous as hell.

It's odorless and tasteless, which means if you spill some in your coffee, you won't realize it until you're dead. A tiny amount of it, if ingested, will kill a human being in a couple of minutes."

"Oh my God. Is it painful—the death I mean?"

"Yes," Meg said, "the death is agonizing. We know this from two accidents in our trials of the product."

"Agonizing death?" I mumbled. "How terrible."

"Could you bring some of the stuff home with you tomorrow? I'd like our quality control people to test it on an empty lot behind headquarters."

"Sure," Meg said, "but promise me you'll follow the safety precautions on the package."

"A user doesn't have to wear a gas mask or something, does he?" I asked.

"No, nothing as heavy duty as a gas mask. A simple surgical mask will do as it says on the package."

"A surgical mask? Something that could be worn underneath something like, I don't know, a burqa or something."

"Do some of your quality control people wear burqas?" Meg asked, a look of amusement on her face.

"Suffolk County farmers come in all sizes and types," I said.

"I'll bring a pound-sized carton with me tomorrow," Meg said. "It comes in two forms, powder and pills. The pills are meant to be placed around weeded areas in the early spring."

"And it's tasteless, I believe you said?"

"Yes, and that adds to its danger. I'll bring a box of powder and a box of pills. Again, make sure your people read the instructions."

CHAPTER FORTY-SEVEN

I'm just one of the guys, the thought occurred to me as I sat at the conference table at the FBI New York Headquarters at 26 Federal Plaza in Manhattan. I was there for yet another status meeting on the terror attacks using my company's robots. The usual people were at the meeting, including Rick Bellamy from the FBI, Buster from the CIA, Dr. Bennie Weinberg, detective and shrink, and me. They had gotten used to having Mike in their meetings, and my being there didn't cause any concern. They treated me just like a fellow government investigator.

I wasn't, of course.

"There's going to be a high level ISIS meeting next Tuesday," Buster said.

"Where?" Rick Bellamy asked.

"That ISIS safe house in Tenafly, New Jersey. I've got one of my inside guys planting bugs all over the place. We're not going to raid the place, of course, because we don't have any grounds for arrests, but it will be a great source of intelligence. Soon they're going to find out that the safe house isn't safe."

"What's the address in Tenafly?" Rick asked.

"It's 711 Sycamore Street," Buster said.

"I've been in that neighborhood before," I said. "Nice area. That's 711 Sycamore Street, yes?" I said as I jotted down the address. "Will that guy Mahmood be there?" I asked out of curiosity.

"We don't know," Bellamy said. "We hope he will be because we have some inside information that he may be the kingpin behind their whole exploding robot operation."

⟞⟊ ⟋⟝

On my way home, I told Roady to pull into the parking lot of the local dry cleaners so I could pick up my clothes.

"Hi, Jenny. Had a religious conversion recently?" Stacy, the store owner asked, chuckling.

"What are you talking about?"

"There's a black burqa in your stuff. I wanted to ask you if it's yours."

"Oh, yeah," I mumbled. "Costume party for a friend this Saturday. Don't you think I'll look pretty?"

"Beats the hell out of me how a woman could wear something like this," Stacy said. "You can't even tell who's wearing it, whether it's a man or a woman."

A wonderfully functional garment, I thought. And it promotes modesty.

CHAPTER FORTY-EIGHT

"Good afternoon, ladies and gentlemen, I'm Shepard Smith for Fox News. There continues to be startling developments in the world of terror, or should I say the management of the world of terror. Last night 12 ISIS members were killed at what the FBI describes as an ISIS safe house in Tenafly, New Jersey. The men died a grisly death, having been poisoned with a powerful pesticide. A person wearing a burqa was seen running from the house. I have with us on the phone, Agent Richard Bellamy of the FBI. Please tell us, Agent Bellamy, do these deaths have anything in common?

"We think the deaths may be the result of internal disputes," Bellamy lied. "The people killed were all high level ISIS operatives, many of whom we've been tracking for years."

"Agent Bellamy, the deaths were caused by a poison that inflicts horrible suffering before the victim dies. Does that tell you anything about the perpetrator or perpetrators?"

"Shepard," Bellamy said, "whoever did this was angry—very angry."

CHAPTER FORTY-NINE

"Rick, I think you should turn on the TV," Bellamy's assistant, Barbara, said.

"Good morning, ladies and gentleman, Wolf Blitzer here for CNN. I don't know if this is a follow-up report or a new story. Yesterday we reported on a gruesome killing of 12 Middle Eastern men, who authorities suspected of being radical Islamists. They were all poisoned by an odorless and tasteless pesticide that was mixed in their food at dinner. Just minutes ago we received anonymous tip that four men were gunned down as they entered a mosque in lower Manhattan. According to a police officer at the scene, the bullet casings indicate that the weapon used was an AR-15, a semi-automatic assault rifle similar to an AK-47. I've just been told that the four men were on the watch list of the Department of Homeland Security. We have no details as to motive and no suspects have been arrested."

CIA agent Buster and Dr. Ben Weinberg walked into Bellamy's office for a scheduled meeting.

"Wolf Blitzer is just wrapping up a report about four Middle Eastern guys who were shot with an AR-15 as they walked into a mosque," Rick said. "This is getting interesting, guys."

"Hey, check it out," Buster said, pointing to the TV. "Blitzer's got more."

"These developing stories are getting more and more curious by the minute," Blitzer said. "We've just received news of three more Arab-looking men being killed, this time by a machete- wielding assailant. The men were entering their car at a parking garage in Queens when they were attacked. One eyewitness said they saw a woman wearing the traditional Islamic robe called a burqa, which completely obscures a woman's face. To be accurate, we don't know if the assailant was a woman, because men have been known to wear a burqa as camouflage. The fact that one assailant killed three grown men adds to the idea that the assailant may have been male, or an extremely athletic female."

Blitzer was walking across the sound stage when he grabbed his right ear and said,

"Wait, there's more. I've just gotten word that the body of Farouk Mahmood, a widely sought-after terror suspect, was found lying in the driveway of his home in Queens. He was decapitated, and his head and a bloody axe were found next to his body."

Blitzer then began to wrap up the reports and put them in perspective. He continued to hold his right ear, as if he was expecting more reports from his producer.

"From a criminal investigation perspective, it's been a shocking 48 hours," Blitzer said. "Since the poisoning of a dozen men two nights ago to today's body count, the authorities, including the NYPD, the FBI, and even the CIA have been trying to get a handle on what's going on. Twenty men have been killed, and every one of them was on the Terror Watch List of the Department of Homeland Security. As FBI agent Rick Bellamy told us two days ago, 'Whoever did this was angry—very angry.' "

CHAPTER FIFTY

I magine yourself at a happy social function. People are talking, laughing, and dancing. The band is playing your favorite songs. It's loud as hell, but a wonderful, happy kind of loudness. You have a sense that everything in the world is doing just fine. Then the music stops, as does the talking, laughing, and dancing. A door swings open and a freezing cold breeze wafts in. Then there's silence.

I want to stop having that nightmare, but what I want doesn't seem to be happening. Mike was the biggest part of my life. He's the happy part of my recurring dream, the part that makes the world seem bright. Now he's dead.

Until two days ago, I was the most law abiding person you could meet. I never even strayed more than five miles over the speed limit when I drove. I believe in order, and that means obeying the law first and foremost. That was me. Forty-eight hours ago.

CHAPTER FIFTY-ONE

"I have a word completion quiz." Bennie Weinberg said. "The enemy of my enemy is…"

"My friend," both Buster and Rick Bellamy answered.

"After the events of the past few days," Bennie said," it seems like the government's case files on ISIS in the United States has gotten a lot smaller. The people we were tracking and planning to arrest are dead, all within 48 hours. You said it best when you were interviewed on TV, Rick. You said, and I remember it clearly, 'Whoever did this was angry—very angry.' "

"So where does this leave us," Buster said. "Somebody saved us a lot of trouble. So what? We're neither judges nor jurors, we're law enforcement people. We've got to find out who the murderer is."

"And what do we do when we find him?" Bennie asked. "Give him a medal? He, whoever he is, killed a bunch of mass murderers, people who targeted children. Somebody killed the enemy. That makes him our friend as far as I'm concerned."

"And I think you know who it is, Ben," Buster said.

"Rick, Jenny Bateman is here. She said you were expecting her."
The receptionist said

When I walked in, all three men stood.

Bellamy, who likes to get right to the heart of the matter, spoke first.

"Jenny," said Bellamy. "We'd like to know if you have any thoughts to share about the recent deaths of the radicals."

"I plan on going to church this afternoon to light a candle for the poor dears. I just hope they didn't suffer too much."

"Anything you'd like to say, Jenny?" Buster said.

"What is there to say?" I asked. "Twenty fucking savage animals are dead. That makes your jobs easier, freeing up your time to concentrate on other files. It also makes my job of running Robot Depot easier, because my products won't be used to slaughter innocent people."

None of them spoke. They sat in silence as if they were waiting for a meeting to begin.

"If you guys think that I committed those murders, good fucking luck," I said. "First you'll need to find the evidence, then you'll need to find 12 jurors who would convict me. That's right, you need to find 12 people who will hear all about the butchers, including the scumbag who decapitated my husband. I'm sure they'd love to find me guilty, not that I had anything to do with it, of course. Unless you guys have something more important to talk to me about, I have a meeting on Wall Street in a few minutes."

I walked out of Rick's office and closed the door behind me. I heard it open again, turned around, and saw Bennie Weinberg walking toward me.

"Jen, a minute of your time, please," Bennie said.

I'd gotten to think of Bennie like a brother, and no way in hell would I turn down a request from him to talk to me.

"Jenny, you know who did it. I know who did it," Bennie said. "Remember, I'm 'Bennie-the- Bullshit-Detector?' So I just have one suggestion. Please keep your mouth shut. Rick and Buster are duty bound to arrest anyone they reasonably suspect to be the killer."

"Bennie, you were there at Yankee Stadium with me and Mike," I said. "You saw what those savages did to a crowd of innocent people. The same kind of drone attack happened to a bunch of children at a sailing regatta out on Long Island. Children, Bennie, *children*. I'm not saying I had anything to do with it, of course, but what would *you* do if you had to opportunity to administer some justice?"

"You pose a tough question, Jen," Bennie said, "but please do as I ask and keep your mouth shut."

"Ben," I said, "You didn't answer my question. Remember that cute little girl at Yankee Stadium who had her arm blown off? She bled to death on your lap. So I ask you, as one combat veteran to another, what would you have done to the enemy if you had the opportunity?"

"Jenny, I'm a doctor and a detective, I..."

"I didn't ask you for a fucking resume, Bennie, I asked you what you would have done to the scumbags if you had the chance."

"I would have killed every last one of them," Bennie said, letting go of a deep sob and wiping tears from his eyes.

"Case closed, doctor, as far as I'm concerned. Be well, my friend."

I walked to the elevator as Bennie went back to Rick's office. I turned and saw him wiping tears from his eyes again and blowing his nose as he reached for the door handle. I should feel nervous but I'm not. I don't give a shit what they think. Mike's dead, and the only thing that keeps me from completely cracking up is that his killers are dead too. Not that I had anything to do with it.

"So what have we got," Rick Bellamy said after Bennie returned to the room. "Do you think Jen Bateman is the enemy of our enemy?"

"And what if she is?" Bennie asked, his voice raised. "What would that mean?"

"Yeah, yeah, I know," Bellamy said, rubbing his hands against his face in frustration. "It means that she's our friend."

CHARACTERS – *ROBOT DEPOT*

Angus – Android robot
Bateman, Jenny – College Professor and Mike's wife
Bateman, Mike – CEO, Robot Depot
Beekman, John – Dissatisfied robot owner
Bellamy, Rick – FBI Agent
Bliedner, Dennis – TV Reporter
Brody, James – John Beekman's first attorney
Buono, Walter – Terrorist bomber
Buster — CIA agent
Carly — A self-driving car
Cavuto, Neil – TV Commentator, himself
Clayton, George – Police Commissioner, New York City
Dick – Greeter at Robot Depot headquarters
Dusty — A floor cleaning robot
Flager, Jim –Terrorist bomber
Fleming, Nancy – Assistant to Chuck Walsh at the Jameston Building
Francine – Robot receptionist
Fuller, Brian – Medical Director of Columbia Presbyterian Hospital
Gentile, Bob – Defense lawyer
Jackson, Billy – Chief scientist, Robot Depot

Knight, Dianne – Receptionist
Livingston, George – Quality control engineer
Mahmood, Farouk – ISIS leader
Mujahedeen, Ali – Assistant to Farouk Mahmood
Omelet — A cooking robot
Stroud, Matt – Host, TV Show, *The Book*
Townsend, Phil – Robot Depot legal counsel
Walsh, Chuck – Manager of the Jameston Building
Weill, Nigel – Pseudonym for famous author
Weinberg, Bennie - Detective and psychiatrist
Whiteacre, Blanche – Public Relations Executive
Winston, Jack – Quality control engineer
Yaeger, Wally – Personal Injury lawyer

THE BOOKS OF RUSS MORAN

All books are available on Amazon.com, and also as ebooks on The Kindle.

The Gray Ship – **Book One of** *The Time Magnet Series*
http://amzn.to/16GPumH
"This provocative, intensely powerful novel is a must-read for sci-fi fans and Civil War aficionados, though mainstream fiction readers will find it heart-rending and inspiring as well. A rare read that's not only wildly entertaining, but also profoundly moving."
— Kirkus Reviews

The Thanksgiving Gang – **Book Two of** *The Time Magnet Series*
http://amzn.to/1NzBs7N
"I had never read a book before written in an efficient, minimalistic prose... Instead of writing what most readers want to read, he gives voice to life-like characters, with their flaws and prejudices. They are not infallible superheroes. It's always nice to find a new voice in fiction and to enjoy creativity at its best." — C. Ludewig.
"Breakneck pacing and virtually nonstop action" – Kirkus Reviews

A Time of Fear – Book Three of *The Time Magnet Series*
http://amzn.to/1zdjaG9
"His story is fascinating, and adds even more depth to this already cavernously deep novel. Amazingly unique, chilling and well written, Moran weaves a future that is both desperate and hopeful. Blending modern fears with science fiction results in a tale that will keep you reading long into the night." Five stars!" —Heather

The Skies of Time – Book Four of *The Time Magnet Series*
http://amzn.to/1CCC3jg
In *The Skies of Time*, you will recognize the two main characters, Ashley Patterson, now an admiral, and her husband, Jack Thurber. They met and fell in love in *The Gray Ship*, and now they're in for the adventure of their lives in *The Skies of Time*. Ashley and Jack have been such prominent characters in all four books of The Time Magnet Series that I feel like they're old friends. You will also recognize some of the other characters. But if I told you who they are, it would ruin the fun.

"I'm big fan of this series and this one may be the best. I hope there is another book to this series since it keeps getting better. There are a few questions I have about certain events that makes the next one even more suspenseful. These are great books to binge read one after the other." — Time Travel Fan

The Shadows of Terror – Book One of the *Patterns Series*
http://amzn.to/1IDQzJS
A novel that explodes off the front page of your newspaper.

Terrorism now has a new face, a face that's obscured in the shadows. The radical forces of destruction have learned to make themselves invisible to the West, and preventing a terrorist attack has become almost impossible.

A new war has begun, World War III.

Rick Bellamy, an FBI agent who specializes in counterterrorism, is engaged in his own war, a war with no end.

Bellamy's wife, Ellen, a prominent architect, discovers that she's in the middle of the greatest terror plot to date.

To defeat the enemy, Bellamy first has to uncover the clues, to shine a light on the shadows. He has to find patterns – before it's too late.

"Move over James Patterson and Mary Higgins Clark. There's a new guy in town. Russ Moran's new book – *The Shadows of Terror.*" — Frank from Lynbrook

The Scent of Revenge, - Book Two in the *Patterns Series.* http://amzn.to/1UvDRmw

The world is at war – World War III. FBI Agent Rick Bellamy and his wife, Ellen, find themselves in the middle of a sinister terror plot.

Someone is attacking young prominent women, inflicting a horrible disease.

Nobody knows its origin, nobody knows how to stop it, nobody knows how to cure it.

Rick Bellamy and a team of scientists want to go on offense. But how?

Will the lives of the women be changed forever? When will the attacks stop?

"Heart pounding, can't put down thriller that will force you to look at terrorism in different light. Life in America will never be the same." —Cold Coffee Cafe

Sideswiped - Book One in the Matt Blake series of legal thrillers. http://amzn.to/1MkxX35

Trial lawyer Matt Blake took on a perfect case.

It involved a sideswipe collision in which his client's husband, an investigative reporter, was killed. The evidence of negligence was overwhelming. Eyewitnesses testified that defendant was talking on his cell phone when he hit the other car.

But was it negligence? Was it an accident?

Or was it murder?

Matt uncovers evidence that the act may have been intentional. Somebody wanted the man silenced. Somebody wanted the man dead.

Somebody had a lot to hide.

The signs started to point to the highest levels of government.

An open-and-shut personal injury case suddenly became a vast conspiracy of terror.

"This book hooks you in from the first line. *Sideswiped* draws you into the world of Matt Blake and you become emotionally attached to him and his journey. The story itself is so well-written and moves quickly so there is never a dull moment." —Sarah Elle

"Moran demonstrates the depth of his writing talent by developing a new genre with *Sideswiped*, a legal thriller. Branching out from his previous novels dealing with time travel, Moran goes in a whole new direction with Book One in the Matt Blake series. He creates a wild but totally believable story of modern day intrigue and suspense. Moran also deftly weaves into this book some of my favorite characters from his prior novels. I am looking forward to starting Book #2 - *The Reformers* — Frank from Lynbrook on August 16, 2016

The Reformers - Book Two of the Matt Blake series of legal thrillers, is the sequel to *Sideswiped.*
http://amzn.to/2m8uMdu
The forces of radical Islam are on the run.

Their leadership has been decimated, their ranks thinned, their power disappearing by the week.

Their recruiting efforts have been cut off, the radical websites shut down, and the attraction of jihad is losing its appeal among the young.

With targeted assassinations, military strikes, as well as the loss of oil fields and gold mines, radical Islam is fast losing power.

But who is responsible?

It isn't the United States Government. It's a new force the world has never seen before.

Lawyer Matt Blake and his wife Diana find themselves in the middle of the most gigantic plot the world has ever seen, a conspiracy that's only begun to grow.

"I've been a fan of the author, Russell Moran, since reading *Sideswiped* a few months ago, so I admittedly went into this book with quite high expectations. That being said, I had no idea that "*The Reformers*" was going to play out in the way that it does and I can see myself giving this book a re-read in the future. In fact, I am even more impressed by the storyline of this read than the last and it has left me excited to see more." Lucidity.

The Keepers of Time – Book Five of the Time Magnet Series
http://amzn.to/2wjVSTt

Admiral Ashley Patterson and her husband Jack have done it again. They've traveled through time, 200 years into the future—aboard a nuclear aircraft carrier, Ashley's flagship.

They discover a new world, a strange new world—a post-nuclear war world—one that is both a beacon of hope, and a cry of despair.

They meet a group of people who call themselves *The Keepers of Time,* an organization dedicated to preserving history and culture.

But the world around them has harkened back to a primitive and savage past, one that includes human sacrifice.

Ashley knows they have to have to get back to the present to warn the government of the unspeakable horrors that await.

But finding the way back to the present is their greatest challenge, an almost insurmountable one.

"A wild time travel yarn that starts fast and doesn't slow down until the end."

A Reunion in Time
http://amzn.to/2tneIsg

What if a 37-year-old adult travels back 20 years in time and finds himself in high school, followed by his 36-year-old wife? They're now teenagers, 17 and 16.

Adults in teenage bodies, they struggle to convince the people from their past that they are real, not apparitions. With the benefit of hindsight, they know the history of the past 20 years, and it isn't pretty.

Rick and Ellen are married, and now have to adjust to married life as teenagers in 2001. Rick is a senior FBI official and Ellen is a famous architect.

But everybody sees them as kids. Nobody believes that they're married, and nobody believes their stories—until Rick and Ellen predict 9/11.

How do they find their way back to the year they came from? How do they warn the authorities of the cataclysm that will occur in the future? The answer is to find the time portal—the wormhole—that brought them to 2001. But the site has changed. It's no longer the place where they crossed the wormhole. Will they live out the balance of their lives beginning as teenagers? "We've all wish we could go back to earlier times with the mind we have now. This Russell Moran book takes you there and it is a fun creative Romp well worth reading. *A Reunion in Time* is highly recommend!" Kindle Customer.

The President is Missing – Book Three of the Matt Blake series.
http://amzn.to/2t9v7wu

While he was addressing the nation from a submerged nuclear submarine, President Blake's message is suddenly cut off. Anyone listening heard an explosion. The explosion was followed by floating debris five minutes later.

First Lady Dee Blake has doubts, which she shares with naval high command and the new president. She thinks the explosion and the debris were a ruse to make people think the sub was destroyed, and her husband with it.

Could the sub have been hijacked and the president kidnapped?

But who would commit such an act? What is its purpose?

Was it Russia, China, Iran, or a shadowy group of freelance terrorists?

The new president appoints Dee as his Chief of Staff, with explicit instructions to find the missing submarine—and President Matt Blake.

Her life, and the life of the nation, suddenly take a horrifying turn.

Robot Depot, the book you've just read, is Russ Moran's latest book, published in
September, 2017. Look for *The Maltese Incident*, a two-million year time travel adventure, coming in October of 2017. In November, 2017, *A Climate of Doubt,* a book that looks at the horrors of climate change, will be launched. It's Book Three of the Matt Blake Series. Matt and Dee Blake take on their biggest challenge to date.

If you enjoyed *Robot Depot*, please consider leaving a brief review on amazon.com. Reviews are an author's lifeblood.

ABOUT THE AUTHOR

Russ Moran is the author of 12 novels. *The Gray Ship*, Book One of *The Time Magnet* series, is a story of time travel, alternate history, romance, and a nuclear warship that finds itself in the Civil War. *The Thanksgiving Gang* is the sequel, *A Time of Fear* is Book Three, *The Skies of Time* is Book Four, and *The Keepers of Time* is book five.

The Shadows of Terror is Book One of The Patterns series, followed by *The Scent of Revenge*.

A Reunion in Time is a time travel novel, but not in the Time Magnet series.

Sideswiped, a legal thriller, is Book One of the Matt Blake Series.

The Reformers is Book Two of the Matt Blake Series, and *The President is Missing* is Book Three.

Robot Depot, is a novel about our automated future.

Moran also published five nonfiction books: *Justice in America: How it Works—How it Fails; The APT Principle: The Business Plan That You Carry in Your Head; Boating Basics: The Boattalk Book of Boating Tips; If You're Injured: A Consumer Guide to Personal Injury Law; How to Create More Time.* He's a lawyer and a veteran of the United States Navy. He lives on Long Island, New York, with his wife, Lynda.

www.ingramcontent.com/pod-product-compliance
Lightning Source LLC
Chambersburg PA
CBHW070114260626
47160CB00004B/1469